MW00939605

Also by Valerie Rene'a

Naked Tales

Also by Nayr Rashad

Chocolate Desires: Carmel Sheets

Women of the White Rose

The Journey of My Words

Scarlet Roses

The Black Love Challenge

hidden desires

FROM THE CREATIVE MINDS OF
VALERIE RENE'A NAYR RASHAD

When Giyani and Everett Cooper decided to embark on a sexual conquest to keep their marriage spicy, things were great. They had a few rules that were in place that the respect of the union was never compromised. Everett is a Defensive coordinator for the USC Trojans, he took on where his father left off, coaching. Giyani (Yani) is a sexual marriage guru as well as a yoga instructor. The two worked together perfectly to create a beautiful marriage, although their past was bumpy almost causing Yani her life.

Things were perfect until a trip to paradise started a rocky road for the young couple. Being together since they've met in college, they've been virtually inseparable. Only time will tell if the issues that arise can be conquered by them, on their way to a peaceful union.

Read as plots thicken and sexual tension maxes out. Complete with back and forth, non-stop action. This attention grasping novel will have you wanting more and more and just when you think you can't take it another twist is thrown your way. Fall in love with the characters and story. Get upset, cry, feel, get hot and bothered, and become one as you take the journey with Yani and Everett.

Contents

Excerpt from Carnal Waves: Surviving the Storm

...all secrets aren't good secrets

Aloha

He looked over to see her small frame as she walked into the bathroom; he then turned to the alarm clock. It was only 7:25 and they already had two amazing sessions. She peeped from behind the door, looked at him and winked. Then she giggled at his current state, they'd traded blows back and forth throughout the day trying to get the better of each other. She won this battle as he laid there, his member layered with her juices. They were on vacation in Hawaii, staying at the Mauna Lani Resort on Big Island.

It was their anniversary, eight years of blissful matrimony. Eleven if you count the years they dated in college. Everett proposed after the

1

final game of the season, in front of thousands of fans so Yani never questioned his devotion. They had a small wedding on the beach with their family and a few close friends from college. The setting was euphoric. Family and friends sat along the white sand beach that cascaded across the land. A small breeze offered a slight chill as the sun began to set and reflect its light off the waves that crashed along the shore.

White roses created the path that Yani walked down to meet her husband to be while the tunes of soft music played in the background by a local jazz player. Everett eyes lit up as Yani made her way towards him. Tears of joy flowed from her eyes. The warm sand moved through her toes as she approached the altar. The fresh air expanded in Everett's lungs as he took a deep breath and removed Yani's veil. It meant a lot to Everett because his father was able to see that he found a great woman to share his life with. This was one of the values that he instilled into him, "A family man is never a poor man".

Giyani wrapped her locs into a ponytail revealing two hearts on her neck behind her ears; her cocoa skin still gleamed with sweat. She massaged the back of her neck, at the top of her spine was an ankh cross with Everett's name beneath it, usually one of the spots he focus his kisses and nibbles. She had a very thick build but was extremely limber. Yani closed her walnut size eyes tilting her head back and inhaled the pumpkin scented candle that filled the air. The scent reminded her of being back home in the south, with the autumn breeze kissing against her melanin.

Giyani was pure at the time when they first met, only experiencing a bit of kissing. They sexually woke each other, exploring every facet that they could. Last night was no different coercing one of the maids and bellhops assigned to their room to join them for a little fun. Everything was an adventure for them; they never lost interest in each other.

"Yani", Everett bellowed from the bed.

Yani stood in the door frame her nipple piercings gleaming in the sunlight, "Yes my love?"

Everett laid there with a pouty face, his arm draped over his head, with one holding his stomach knowing that would draw her over to him. As soon as she reached the bed, she placed her small hand over his brow checking his forehead; he was fine from what she could see.

When she pulled her hand away he wrapped his large arms around her pulling her on top of him, she giggled uncontrollably as he tickled her. He knew she was very ticklish. He asked her questions as she tried to gain enough breath to speak. He stopped for a second, she tried to escape biting his arm and the chase was on. They sprinted throughout the 3 bedroom villa. He had her cornered, she stated she gave up but he wasn't hearing it, knowing it was just a ploy. He said ok and walked towards her only to tickle her once again under her stretched arms. She giggled and then snorted; he paused then pinched her nose and turned around to head back to the main room they were staying in.

She jumped on his back wrapping her legs around his waist and began to kiss his neck she knew that made him powerless, now it was her turn to ask questions. She made him weak when she kissed his spot, breathing her warm breath against his neck. She felt so soft against him. He reached around grabbing her butt so she couldn't slip off. She kissed once again at his neck, this time running her tongue down it.

"Tell me you love me", says Yani.

Everett started to speak but he couldn't, he dwelled on that kiss of hers. Continuing to walk towards the living area, Everett stopped at the chaise. Yani hopped off and pushed him down. She looked at him masterfully. He gazed in her lustful eyes; it never failed how easily she still turned him on. Their adventurous spirits had them plotting new heights to explore.

As Everett leaned back in the chaise, Yani began to disrobe him. He was at full attention. He looked up at her he gave a slight grin. She knew it was all her doing, so she gave out a devilish giggle.

"How bad do you want me?" asked Yani.

"You already know", he says.

She pushed open his legs as she laid flat on her stomach. He jumped at the insertion into her mouth, it was warm and inviting. His body relaxed as she began to take long suckles at his shaft. His body rocked as she nursed on him. She soaked up the chaise with her saliva while sucking at him in a steady but vigorous motion. His hips raised up giving her every inch.

Yani moaned. She found such pleasure at pleasing Everett. His body danced with her mouth creating erratic motions. He forced her head deep into his lap and listened for the sounds of when his dick touched the back of her throat. But Everett knew she loved when he did that, it made her attack him even more. Yani stood up and looked Everett deep into his eyes, she leaned down and pulled his legs together. She then climbed her way on top of him; the scent of jasmine tickled his nose. He started to reach for her waist but she slapped his hands away. She reached behind herself and spread her cheeks apart and inserted him deep inside her.

They both let out moans as her warmth and moisture surrounded him. She swayed her hips back and forth, resting tightly in his lap. He massaged her insides, hitting each of her love spots as her hands found their way to her breast. She cupped them gently and pulled at her nipples. Everett leaned up to greet them. He scooped up her left breast and placed it in his mouth; he rolled his tongue around her areola. Her skin tasted tangy with a hint of salt. He then began to bite at her nipple gently; Yani gave out a slight purr while still swaying her hips.

Everett was driving her insane with his tactics; her hands went to her breast to finding their way to her locs becoming tangled. Her body began to shake but Everett wasn't having that. He picked her up off of him as if she weighed next to nothing and laid her in her own pool of juices. Sex was a pleasurable competition to them and Everett wasn't about to let her cum yet.

He pressed her legs back until they almost touched the cushion, luckily for her she was limber or he would have torn her in half as he once again dug into her. The stirring sounds of wetness hit his ears as he moved around in her walls, her warmth collapsed around him. Her short powerful legs fought back as he pushed his body weight into her. He plunged thrusting his hips downward, getting on the tips of his toes for leverage. He was waiting for a certain moment, until then he was relentless.

Yani was folded beneath him with her eyes closed, teeth clutched, hands gripping the cushion, "I love you!"

There it was he had her right where he wanted her, he looked down as she creamed on his staff, her eyes now open peering into her lovers eyes and her mouth parted panting breaths as his onslaught continued. He knew what was coming next as her hands pushed into his abdomen. She was getting ready to explode. His rhythm grew faster, his thrust more fierce.

She looked up at her warrior wondering when his stroke would cease, but the fire in her stomach heated up. It was time and right on cue she came. The chaise was drenched. He pulled out and began to suckle at her already purring kitten.

"Baby stop, please", she cried.

His licks were relentless as she continued to orgasm, until his fill was met. He stood up and wiped his mouth and beard with his forearm and turned around to walk away.

Yani called out to Everett as he walked with a grin on his face. She stood to her shaky feet, she walked after him. She caught up with him and pushed him against the wall.

"Where are you going?" she says to him as she grabbed at his rod, stroking it with her right hand.

She kneeled in front of him and slowly caressed him while she looked up into his eyes. She took her tongue run it up his shaft then to his chest until she reached his lips. She placed her tongue between the opening of his mouth and searched for his tongue until they met and became entangled. Everett's dick hardened even more. He placed his hand on the top of her head and pushed her down back to his dick so he could feel her warmth surround him. It was hard and standing upright awaiting the moisture of her mouth with insertion.

Everett tilted his head back while he enjoyed the euphoria of her mouth and its motion.

Saliva started flowing down his shaft as he says a mental prayer "please don't stop!"

She saw the excitement on his face and felt the pulsation between her jaws. His body was speaking to her. She felt her flower leak, because this was also pleasure to her; she gave him the attention that he sought. He put his hands on her chin; he lifted her up and licked the saliva off her lips.

She whispered, "Let me have you, all of you!"

He lifted Yani up off the floor and planted his feet firmly on the ground. Yani found her place on his throne and eased her way down, she rested on his hips. She awaited this moment and released all her tension on top of him, she rocked her hips up and down as he clutched her tightly into his grasp; he pushed up into her deeper and deeper. He gripped her hips, and guided her to the perfect pace, she looked up at him while she bit her lips as if to say; "Like this Daddy?"

Everett moaned his approval; "Yes, don't stop", he says.

They've been at this for what seems like hours and the way her body painted his was finer than the Mona Lisa as he dug deep. Their bodies dripped with sweat; all her efforts have been met as he leaned in forward and whispered in her ear "Yani! Baby you're the best!" all his warm cum squirted up inside her.

Their First Taste

Everett carried Yani to the shower and bathed them both. They got dressed for a night on the Island, first was dinner at CanoeHouse, Yani heard about it from one of her clients. She wore her locs in a bun with a Hibiscus flower to the side. Her body glowed and smelled of peaches from her lotion. A red and yellow sun dress adorned her body; she wore no panties which let her ass sway, though it had firmness to it, it still jiggled when she walked. Everett threw on his Sperry's with his dark tan linen pants and deep brown fitted shirt.

They arrived at the restaurant and were led to their table by a medium height and build waitress. Yani seemed to notice her more than

Everett; his attention was on Yani, her smooth brown skin made his blood thin to his heart and manhood leaving his head to float in her aura. They sat down reminiscing on past stories like a time when they were in the premature dating phase.

Everett said "Do you remember that time we had to spend the night at the hospital?"

Yani gave a sly look and said "Yeah, my ankle still hurts when I think about it."

"You looked so cute in that hospital gown with your ass out" Everett said.

Yani gasped with shock, throwing her lemon from her glass at Everett.

"Shut up!"

Everett laughed "You had me down to my boxers all you had to do was get one more basket."

"I would have if I didn't trip over your size boats" Yani snapped!

14

Everett laughed now but at the time he felt so bad that he spent 2 weeks catering to her every need. It touched her soul, she felt herself falling in love. Afraid of the possible rejection of her feelings, she held them until the first night they shared a small piece of intimacy. While he attended to her ankle, he rubbed it while she looked at him with those large bedroom eyes. With a kiss they shared the most intimate moment two souls could ever share. He was the one to say those special words that melted her heart.

"I love you", Everett whispered in her ear.

She felt heat radiate all over her, she was in love with this man and she knew he felt the same. They had a real love which made their passion even greater.

They both smiled about the past as Everett made a joke about his glass; Yani was still lost while she looked at him, she remembered all the nights she laid on his chest as she curled his beard up in her fingers, while he held a palm full of her derriere. She also thought about the nights she laid on his back, while they watched movies, her nipples hard tickling his back as she kissed his tattoos. She would always feel her kitten moisten beneath her, while she sucked on his neck.

He loved her full pouty lips, the way they danced along his tape line sending tingles throughout his body as she moved closer down his spine. Everett could feel his nature begin to rise beneath him. While she kissed at his neck, she took her tongue and ran it in circles behind his left ear. That was Everett's spot. He turned over, now on his back he grabbed Yani by the face and peered deep into her eyes.

His hands began to roam through her hair as she stared back at him. She leaned in to meet with his ailing lips. Their kiss was full of passion and want. Yani could feel her panties becoming soaked as she wiggled on top of Everett. The time felt right, Yani wanted to give herself completely to Everett because she felt he was so deserving of it. No one had treated her with such care and compassion such as he had.

"I think I'm ready", she said to him.

Everett was shocked, he knew it would happen eventually but he didn't know that it would be now.

"Are you sure?" he asked her.

"Yes..." she said with nervousness in her eyes.

Everett wiggled his way up and gently placed her on her back. He looked down at his queen with a smile on his face. He wanted nothing more than to satisfy her in every way possible.

"I love you", he chanted.

Everett began to remove her pants; he unbuckled them and slowly slide them off to reveal her lace black panties. He then unbuttoned her shirt as she assisted him to get it off. She wore a black bra with pink lace trimmings. Her body was that of an athlete; toned and firm. Her skin was flawless; she had a birthmark that resembled a crescent moon on her inner thigh.

Everett leaned in and inhaled her scent, she smelled of fresh jasmine. He kissed the nape of her neck. He spread her legs apart with his, she let out the sweetest and most innocent moan in his ear. He was so mesmerized by her hunger and he was ready to feed her. Everett took his left hand and removed her panties while still he gave her body warm kisses. She shyly tugged at this sweats and helped him out of them. He pulled her in closer and pressed his hardened rod against her virgin skin.

Everett looked at Yani and could see the fright in her eyes. Everett was to be her first, she didn't know how to move or what pace to go so he had to remind her it was ok, "Don't be afraid baby, I promise to treat you like the delicate flower you are."

Yani's tension subsided, her body was now relaxed. Everett stood up off to the side of the bed and removed his boxers. Yani saw a penis before in a porn movie her roommate tried to get her to watch, but she had never had one grace her presence until now. She was amazed. She looked up at Everett, lost. But he reassured her that he would guide her along the way.

"Are you sure about this?" Everett asked once more.

She shyly nodded yes as she gazed into his eyes.

"Lay back", Everett said.

She did as he instructed, he looked her over. She was every bit as beautiful bare as he imagined. He was more experienced than she but not by much, seeing as he only experienced a woman's touch once, but it was something about her that fueled his confidence. He placed his frame over hers and kissed her lips. He reached over to his pants pocket and pulled out the condom he had in his wallet. After putting it on he slowly guided the head of his member towards her awaiting hole, he pushed through her lips, she gasped and clutched his arms and dug into them with her fingernails. He worked his way into her slow and deep. It was a painful bliss for her. Yani bit into his shoulder to release pressure. The deeper he drove the harder she bit. At one point she thought she would drawn blood.

After a few moments later she felt a burning in her stomach. Her eyes lit up and she had her first ever orgasm. Then she had another. Her stomach was on fire, her wet spot ached, her mind was in bliss and after a few more strokes Everett collapsed onto her. They shared kisses very satisfied, they then got up to clean off.

It was almost laughable the difference between then and their current escapades. They learned it all together. Most of the time it came from Yani and her want to be a therapist, she wanted to explore every sexual aspect, so she had personal experiences to share with her clients. She was a sex/physical therapist as well as a yoga instructor so she always made sure that things were spicy enough to keep Everett's mind on her. She was actually the one that decided they should introduce others in random sexcapades.

They always chose carefully and it was always someone or a couple they found to be attractive. Yani would be the one to initiate it; Everett would just sit back and reap the benefits. They even experimented with an amateur site that allowed them to upload pictures and videos to make a bit of school money on the side. You might have caught some of their stuff, "The Masked Goddess and Her Beast", they made quite a buzz on the underground porn scene. But it was all in fun. They deleted everything once graduation neared. Well, Yani said she did but kept copies and watched them when she's feeling frisky; not knowing Everett watched her as she got her fix at their highlights.

Dinner neared an end when the waitress came to the table. Yani's foot stroked at Everett's lap under the table his dick increasing at her torture. She even flashed her sparkling nipple that caused him to bite his lips. His eyes began to roll not hearing the soft spoken waitress. But Yani did, she enjoyed it. Now she plotted at how to get the waitress she eye fucked the whole time to meet up with them later.

Kawai, the waitress was a beauty. Her skin looked as if it had been kissed by the sun a thousand times. She was exotic, she had long wavy hair that kissed the dimples on her back. Her voice was soothing with a hint of shyness to it and Yani caught on to that. Yani looked up at the waitress and told her she had a beautiful name.

"What does your name mean?" she asked.

"My name means coming from water", she told Yani.

"Interesting. Do you mind getting me some water?" Yani asked

"Sure. Excuse me for moment" said Kawai.

Kawai returned with the water and ask "would you like anything else?"

"Yes, some ice please I'm kinda hot. I apologize for sending you back and forth, I just like to see you come and go, more so come!" Yani smirked.

Kawai looked at Yani and blushed, she excused herself again and returned with the ice and more drinks. Yani still stroked Everett's dick under the table with her foot, as she looked at him and Kawai both. Yani's nipple was still slightly exposed, Kawai got a glimpse of it while she was poured her a glass of Kona Coffee-Tini She admired this beautiful couple. She even became turned on by their playfulness. When she was about to give Everett his drink she saw Yani's foot in his lap and his bulge that pushed through his pants.

"You have been my favorite table tonight"
Smiled Kawai.

"Well, you've been my favorite waitress.
What time do you get off?" Yani asked.

"You're my last table ma'am", said Kawai.

"Don't be so formal, I'm Giyani but you can
call me Yani and this is my husband Everett",
replied Yani.

"It has been a pleasure serving you both"
Kawai said.

Yani smirked, "We're not finished yet but
the entree was delicious".

"If you think the entree was good you
should try our dessert" exclaimed Kawai.

"What would you recommend?" asked Yani.

"I'm sure you would enjoy one of our
sweetest dishes it's packed a lot of island flavor"
Kawai said with a slight grin.

Yani bit her bottom lip and said "I can't wait to taste that."

"I'm pretty sure it would be a dessert you would never forget", said Kawai.

Everett's eyebrows rose as he looked at Yani. Yani had to think of a way to get Kawai to accompany her and Everett back to the Resort. Everett looked at Yani and saw the determination in her eyes. He knew that she was up to something and she wasn't going to stop till has had full grasp of it. Whatever it was that she was up to Everett would have her back.

"Thank you for making our night special, this is for you", said Yani.

Kawai eyes lit up when Yani handed her a $100.

"Thank you!" exclaimed Kawai.

"Do you have a pen?" asked Yani

"Yes", Kawaii said handing Yani a pen

"This is where we're staying, suite 112 you should join us and we can discuss the dessert you mentioned earlier", Yani said slipping her the note.

Kawai retrieved the note from Yani. She then read it and looked lustfully into Yani's eyes without saying a word and walked away.

"So what are you up to?" Everett said.

"I'm always up to something, I just have a taste for something tropical", Yani grinned.

Everett took the last gulp of his drink, got up from his chair walked over to Yani and stood behind her, he ran his hands down the front of her dress cupped her breast and said, "I have a taste for something too", he leaned into her ear, "You".

The Invite

Everett and Yani returned back to their room shortly after their dinner. Everett lit a few candles while Yani started up the Jacuzzi. It had been a long memorable and teasing night so she wanted to relax while she waited to see if Kawai would show up. While the water was filled she poured in bubbles to make it a little more romantic, but she poured a little too much and had more bubbles than she anticipated. She didn't care though; her sometime motto is "the more the merrier!"

Yani's dress hit the floor; her succulent skin graced the candle light. She stepped inside the Jacuzzi, it was hot but she let her body seep into it while gave out a slight purr. Yani turned on the jet streams that caused more bubbles to occur. She allowed the massage water to pulsate against her flesh. It was heaven, she loved a good massage, it almost reminded her of the one she had back home. The music had a therapeutic type of vibe that hit Yani so hard she felt the beat in the water; it was smooth and massaged her soul. Bubbles glazed her skin as she laid back to rest her head while she closed her eyes. Everett was in the kitchen he prepared freshly cut fruit and poured wine to bring his queen.

Everett headed towards the bathroom to join Yani when he heard a knock at the door. He sat down the tray of fruit near the entryway and opened the door. There stood the exotic goddess Kawai. Everett's eyes lit up, he knew that he and Yani were in for a lovely treat tonight. Everett motioned for Kawai to come in. She had on a silk wrap dress that exposed her small hard nipples. Her long curly hair was now up in a bun. Her legs look like butter and Everett stared on; his mouth began to water.

"Follow me", Everett said to Kawai as he continued towards the bathroom.

He pushed open the door it was now a steam filled room, Yani glowed in the water as he looked down at her.

"I have a surprise for you", he said to her.

"What is it", she asked.

"Something tropical", Everett smiled.

Yani grinned with excitement.

"Come in!" He motioned for Kawai to come inside and join them. As she entered she saw Yani soaking in the tub. Yani stood up to greet her. Her lathered curves sparkled as suds rolled down her frame.

"Thank you for coming", Yani said to Kawai.

"How could I resist", Kawai said shyly.

Kawai's big brown eyes lit up when she saw Yani's dripping wet body glow in the dim lights of the candles. Kawai could feel throbbing sensations build up the more she looked at Yani. She felt between her thighs moisten. Everett took a strawberry and fed it to Kawai. Her lips wrapped around it as she bit into it seductively, she knew exactly what she was doing. Her small nipples grew bigger, harder pushing through her silk dress.

Everett leaned down and kissed Yani, his dick growing by the inch. Kawai shyness slowly slipped away as she too leaned in to kiss Yani. Everett began to unwrap Kawai's dress; he slowly pulled it away from her shoulders. Her breasts were firm and perky. He then began to kiss her neck and ran his tongue along the line. She pressed her hand against the wall to sturdy herself as Yani watched on with her fingers as she fondled her protruding clit.

Kawai's hand ran down Everett's chest and entered his boxers she stroked his stiff rod. She couldn't believe how big it was. She helped him out of his pants and let them fall to the floor. His now hard dick has been freed and is upright and massive. He led Kawai to the Jacuzzi with Yani and helped her in. He then stepped back and leaned against the sink to watch his wife and her seducee.

Everett awaited the show that was about to commence and boy could his wife make a blockbuster hit. He tugged at his stiff rod as he watched Yani pluck away at her victim's nipples, while she yelped with pleasure. Everett's eyes never left them. He could see Kawai get turned on even more as she now let her hands roam over Yani's body. She marveled at Yani's body art.

Caught off guard by Yani's strength, Kawai was lifted onto the lip of the tub with her back to Everett. Yani's face disappeared between Kawai's thighs and began to feed on her exotic juices as she lifted her head only to say, "Mmm just like a fruit cup."

She slurped away at her dessert; Kawai's head began to fade backwards. To keep her from falling Everett stood up behind her, her head rested on his stomach. His thick dick rested on her shoulders. He reached down and tugged at her nipples, she whimpered, her pussy on the brink explosion. Everett looked down at his wife put in work, she looked up and smirked.

Kawai's cries rain throughout the room. To silence herself she took a mouthful of Everett. The sides of her mouth watered profusely down to her nipples. Yani looked up once more; she told her husband he had to taste Kawai. Zoned out, she didn't know what happened until Everett had her small frame on his shoulders and licked away at their foreign partner. He backed up to the wall for support. Not to be left out Yani rose out of the tub like a Goddess of love and walks over to them. She drops to a knee and began to ravish at her husband's member.

The faster she sucked, the faster he licked Kawai. Smacking, licking and drooling echoed and in no time Kawai's river poured down Everett's chest, while his wife drained him below. But Everett wanted to please his queen, so he removed Kawai from his shoulders and laid a towel on the floor then carefully laid Yani onto it.

"Come here", Everett's authoritative voice demanded.

Kawai walked to him and awaited instructions "Sit there on her face and don't let her move."

Everett dove between his wife's thighs and began stroking his tongue against her chocolate flesh. He loved pleasing her and could already hear her moans come from her muffled mouth. He then took two fingers and slid one in her ass the other in her pussy. She shook at the pleasure but Kawai sat on her face she couldn't go anywhere. He licked and finger fucked her faster, he could see the energy leave her body as her struggle became mute. She shivered a few times before cumin. But that wasn't what Everett wanted; he wanted everything she had so he didn't stop. Her body was flailing but he was relentless with his torture despite her mumbled pleas.

Even Kawai felt for her, one orgasm, her back began to lift up. Three, Yani's stomach tightened pleading for mercy. Five, she grabbed for any and everything she could reach but she no longer had the strength to grip. By the time he finished Yani was on her sixth orgasm, her frame was limp. He told Kawai to raise, Yani lay sprawled out. She shivered, her stomach rapidly stretched and shrunk. Everett lifted her up and placed her in the water and cleaned her. He was very delicate with her still shivering body. Kawai looked on digging their connection. She watched as Everett caressed Yani's body with each stroke, lathering her, he pushed aside her hair gently running the water down her neck, stroking the rag across her nipples, carefully, he softly cleansed her. She still felt the tingle in her pussy so she knew just how much damage Everett could cause.

"Okay your turn", Everett said to Kawai's surprise.

He gently cleaned her with the same care; after that she dried off she slipped back on her silk dress. Yani threw a robe around her frame still dripped; she then tied it in the front. Yani walked Kawai to the door and gave her one last kiss before she left. As Kawai was left she told Yani about a big luau on Aumoe Kai Island.

"I'm sure that you will thoroughly enjoy! It's done once a year I have a friend that works there, she's very inclined to meeting new people. It's usually invite only but I know she'll enjoy you two" Kawai said exultantly.

"We will see", Yani said as she waved Kawai goodbye.

Yani closed the door and walked her still glowing body to the room where her husband was awaiting her return. She reached the room, and there he was fast asleep. Everett had worn himself out with his great performance. Yani stood over him, admiring his rested body thrown across the big plush bed. She walked over the bar in the room and grabbed a bottle of water; took a sip and proceeded to climb in bed next to her king.

She wrapped his arm around her until it dangled around her frame. He moved for a moment and the positioned himself near Yani. She pushed her derriere against him and snuggled up. She inhaled his pheromones and let it soothe her; the more she breathed in the deeper she drifted until her body collapsed. Yani dozed off quickly, she didn't realize how tired and worn out she was till her body hit the bed.

Mahalo

Yani and Everett had slept so long it was nearly noon when they awoke to the maid knocking on the door to do her usual rounds. As the maid unlocked the door to come in, Yani yelled out they wouldn't need her services at the moment. Yani crawled out of bed and went to the kitchen to make a quick breakfast for her and Everett.

"Baby wake up", she said softly.

Everett opened his eyes and gawked at his naked wife standing over him with a tray of food. She kept it simple; bacon, scrambled eggs and a bagel with cream cheese. She handed it off to him and went back to the kitchen to grab his Orange

Juice. When she came back, he surveyed her as she walked off to the bathroom. He stared at her as he tried to eat his breakfast, watching her as she splashed water on her face to wake herself up.

He observed as she spread toothpaste on her toothbrush. Yani hopped in the shower and let the water caress her body until her skin soaked up the natural peach scented body wash. When she was done, she walked over to the sliding glass door and opened it. It led to a screened in balcony. She then began to do her daily yoga routine. Everett's eyes grew bigger staring at her, as her naked body curved and twisted in all directions.

Everett slid out of bed as quietly as he possibly could, walking over to Yani. He grabbed her from behind and swiftly turned her around laying the most passionate and wanted kiss on her ever, "I love you baby".

Yani was caught back, Everett felt the kiss touched her insides, "Haven't seen you do that in a while after a kiss", Everett boasted.

"Well if you would have brushed your teeth this morning I might have enjoyed it", Yani joked.

Everett stood there stunned, "Oh yeah? That's how you feel? That's why your legs dangle on the bar stool"

Yani's arms folded she hated when he made jokes about her small stature, "You can kiss my short ass hot breath"

"You are so nasty, horny little leprechaun", Everett laughed as Yani began to ball her fist.

Yani walked up on Everett looking up, "Well baby you must love my lucky charms, because you always clean your bowl".

"I said you were short, I didn't say you weren't magically delicious", Everett joked back.

"You are so lame go take a shower", Yani said pushing him into the bathroom.

Everett smiled as he turned on the shower, "So what are we going to do tonight baby?"

"Well, there is that luau on Aumoe Kai Island. You know the one that Kawai suggested. I mean she did say if we attended she would make sure it would be a great time", Yani said

"Sounds like a plan baby I like it, it's our last night. Let's end it with a bang", Everett yelled over there shower water.

Yani inhaled the scent of the body wash that filled her nose along with the steam from Everett's shower, "Baby hurry up or else we won't be making it out of the house".

As the term implies while in Rome do as the Romans, Yani and Everett dressed as if they were part of the local community. They were prepared for the day as they departed from the villa. They hopped in the red Dodge Challenger and drove into town. Yani released her hair and let her locs hang. She then stuck her foot out the window and relaxed it on the side view mirror and door. Her dress came up to mid-thigh and exposed her tattoos.

Everett gazed over trying to focus on the road, but he knew there was nothing under the dress she wore. He found his hand massage her thighs. He then tip toed his fingers found her wet spot. She let out the moans he loved to hear. His foot accelerated on the gas the more she moaned, things began to blur on the side of them until she exploded. His large fingers were drenched with her juices. She grabbed his hand and licked it clean and then she let him taste her off her lips as the car returned to regular speed. They arrived at the small line of shops, she took some wipes from her purse and cleaned herself up.

They stopped at a shop that sold women's clothing. Yani marveled at the beautiful fabrics and colors. Everett just sat back smiled at his queen. He thought of how lucky he was every time he saw the scar on her back arm. She drove with her roommate back from a party when a pickup truck smashed into them, her roommate died on impact, but Yani survived being pulled to safety, she suffered a few minor scars and the big one that would be with her forever.

She really wasn't the same after that day. She started just living instead of being the cautious virgin she was before. With everything she changed her perspective on life she was just existing and not living, she was afraid of death. But that was in the past, skydiving, snorkeling, rocking climbing, you name it she was willing to try it and Everett was with her the whole way.

The anxiety consumed her before she met with a therapist that unleashed her joy once more. She was tired, tired of the medicine, tired of the fear. But she changed, for the better in her eyes. It helped her take the leap of faith in herself and owning her own business, even when her family felt she was wasting her potential.

It also made her make another life choice. She and her roommate were supposed to take the natural hair journey together. So when she died Yani decided to honor her by making the big chop a few days later. She's been natural ever since. Everett actually helped with it using his own clippers and made sure that it was done with love. Although she was going to do it regardless his support meant the world to her.

Yani began to walk further into the shop, "Don't go too far now", Everett yelled out.

Yani looked back and smiled. She picked up a purple aloha dress and held it at her frame, with a nod from Everett she was sold.

They stopped by an elderly woman who was selling hair flowers; she looked up with the most innocent smile. The couple held hands as she searched through her fresh bucket of flowers before picking one and giving it Yani. It was a beautiful purple hibiscus with a fuchsia center. Everett reached for the money to give to the woman but she refused. She grabbed the couples hand and placed the flower in the cusp their hands. Yani teared up, she was the emotional type.

Everett smiled holding his wife before speaking to the elderly woman, "Mahalo!"

The woman smiled, nodded and the couple walked off. They came across a few shops, they snapped pictures, laughed and enjoyed the scenery. Everett wanted to do one more thing before they left, get a tattoo. They went to a tattoo shop mostly known only by natives to get what would seem to be the lost art of tattooing by an artist like no other. Keone Nunes specialized in the traditional Polynesian art of tapping, which he would dip the moli, a tattoo tool in the pa'u, which was the ink and place it on the skin and tapped. His work was beautiful and Everett thought it would be perfect for them.

When they arrived they were greeted humbly and asked specific questions about the body art they were interested in. They both chose the arm, getting medium sized sleeves with the time frame they had. The work was detailed and perfect, and for Yani it was a moment she would never forget as her empty arm that only possessed a scar, now had a beautiful blooming Hibiscus flower. The couple thanked for his work, it neared time for them to go to the Luau, so they flew to the resort, I mean fashionably late wasn't their style.

Once they arrived back at the resort, they hurried to the room to shower and change clothes. To save time, Yani and Everett washed up together. He loved the way the water would drench her body as she lathered it up with soap, he studied it as it glid across each of her curves. He squeezed more soap into a sponge and washed her back, running it across her ass cheeks, observing it jiggle as he went over each hump. Yani was so relaxed by his caring hands, Everett's dick began to harden but he knew time was of the essence, so he just turned Yani around gave her a kiss on the forehead and continued to wash himself. After they concluded their bath they rinsed off and got out of the shower.

Yani oiled up her body in some mango and coconut oils she had got from the street vendor in town. Her body shimmered. She then twisted her locs up in a bun and placed the purple hibiscus flower on the side of her bun, her beauty exuded. Everett stood there as he gawked and hungered over his beautiful gift God had granted him the pleasure of being in his life. Yani picked up her purple aloha dress and slid it over her silk skin.

"Wow, you look amazing", Everett said to Yani as he watched her get dress.

Yani blushed trying to finish getting dressed, "Thank you baby"

Everett kept it simple, he wore a tank top with some Bermuda shorts and some flip flops that he had picked up from one of the shops in town. It neared time to leave so Everett picked up the keys and headed to the door, but not before he called out to Yani let her know it was time to go. She quickly put on her lavender diamond earrings and hurried off to her husband. Everett handed Yani her flip flops and off they went.

Everett opened the passenger door and bowed as he let his wife in, she laughed saying, "thank you sir." Her scent drifted into his nose and as he closed the door he floated around to the driver's side. They strap themselves in, Everett grabbed for her seat belt to put it on, he felt her soft flesh, his dick hardened. Her smell still warmed his loins. He kissed her twice on the neck, then the cheek, lips and shoulder, then retreated back to his side. Yani knew she was irresistible to him, his bulge thickened in his shorts. Yani got ideas, naughty ideas.

"You know what I love about when you drive baby? I get to torture you and you can't do shit about it", Yani said as she eyed Everett, her eyes glowed with seduction.

Everett gulped as the car moved along, he knew she was right, "Yep, that's right, I can grab your dick just like this and stroke it and stroke it and stroke it", Yani moaned during her mantra, Everett tried his best to keep focus.

"Mmm, my man, my wonderful man, with his thick dick that makes me spiral in the sheets and gets me right together. Ain't that right daddy?" Yani mocked Everett's poetic play on words while she gripped his rod that's now at full attention, "I bet that dick is just waiting and yearning to lay inside mama's warm oven and get baked until it's cream filling shoots out everywhere!"

The car swerved a little as Everett tried to compose himself as she continues, "Or maybe it misses my lips, that kiss it oh so softly, caressing it until it feels the texture of my tongue, then sensations of saliva, coating it in a pleasurable bath. Your pre-cum tempting me to want more of you".

"Fuck!" Everett yelled.

"That's right baby fuck, my, throat", Yani said as she whipped Everett's dick out and begin rapidly sucking away at it, as she slurped, jacked and begged for Everett's warm liquid.

Everett groaned as he looked down to see his wife masterfully strum at his flute, she stirred up songs, hummed lyrics. This album would be platinum if it was up to her. She spoke to it, Everett was in bliss. It was hers of course she knew exactly what to do with it. She knew every vein, curve, the texture, his staff roared but she knew how to bring him to a gentle purr. It hit the back of her throat she gagged a little but she knew she could take more. She tried to swallow him, Everett's eyes rolled. It was coming to that time: The final act, the finale, the End, the climax. The snares began to rip a steady roll; the bass gave a constant rhythm. The orchestra began to rise as his hips rocked, louder, louder, the percussion roared. Crescendos, clash, the bass could no longer be heard, only the ringing of chimes and bells. It was a drowning silence and then the eruption, the culmination of her show was met with a thunderous applause of sporadic breathing. No bow was needed as she removed her mouth to a standing ovation.

The car was back to its steady pace, Yani looked up at the mirror and fixed her lipstick, she placed a kiss on Everett's cheek, then wiping away the lipstick from his face. The place wasn't much further they could already smell the salty sea filled air. Yani began taking self-pictures, then a few with Everett as he was still trying to recover. She turned on the video and danced in her seat, she was an excellent dancer. They found a spot to park and got out. Everett's legs were a bit weak at first but he got himself together and they walked up to the beach.

Luau

The island was beautiful, even at night you could still see a little blue of the sea, the moons reflection kissed the water and danced along the waves. The breeze was sweet scented although it carried a salty mixture, their noses played between the fragrance of food and the tropical air. Bonfires were set along the beach while mellow music blessed the atmosphere. The women were beautiful and the men were just as handsome. The scene was very inviting, they mingled and they laughed, they drank and then drank some more. Yani and Everett had become very loose and so did everyone else on the islands.

Everyone danced and had a great time, even the food was amazing. Everett caught Yani staring into the bonfire, she thought it was so sensual the way the fire begin to heat her skin as she thought of her and Everett's ride down to the island a mere few hours ago. A young lady walked over to them and introduced herself.

"Mahalo, you must be Yani and Everett? I'm Kai, Kawai said to look out for you two."

"Yes, you are correct", said Yani

"Kawai requested that I made sure you two have a great time on your last night here, so I have a bungalow reserved for you. Follow me please!" she insisted.

They followed Kai to a bungalow that was draped in white. Inside was lined with plush pillows and candle light. There was a bottle of wine and white chocolate covered strawberries and apples. There also sat on the table wine glasses. Yani became aroused just sitting there in suspense of what was to happen next. Kai told them that she would be right back and she had one more surprise for them. Everett looked at his wife and placed his fingers on her lips inserting one. He was still slightly hard from being in such a magical state of bliss, something about tonight excited him.

As Yani sucked at his index finger in walked Kai with the most beautiful woman either of them has ever seen. Well besides Yani of course.

"This is Nohea, she and I are here to satisfy you for the remainder of the night", says Kai.

Everett looked at Yani surprised; Kawai had given them a gift after their exciting night together. The couple wasn't expecting this form of escapades, just a fun night with maybe a little fun between themselves. But they wouldn't shy away from this opportunity. Kai closed the curtains and smiled at Nohea, nodding her head.

Nohea stepped further into the bungalow and dropped her silk see through bohemian dress.

There she was a goddess with green eyes, long black hair that rested on her tailbone with chestnut brown skin. Kai followed suit, she dropped her dress and released her full supple breast that made Yani's mouth water. The two girls stood there for a second holding hands awaiting direction.

Yani grabbed the wine and poured everyone a glass toasting to the last night of their vacation, she requested that they make it their most memorable moment yet to date. After the cheers, they placed the glasses down. Yani walked over to the girls while Everett leaned back deeper into the plush pillows. Yani reached out both hands and placed each between the girls legs and commence to glide her fingers across their lower lips. Everett began to release his dick from his pants.

Yani walked around and slapped them both on the ass. Kai jumped at the pleasure slap. They all had beautiful bodies and Everett just sat and enjoyed they view while stroking his fully erect staff. Yani turned the girls towards each other and pushed their heads together to meet in a kiss. Yani's hands still roamed over their bronze bodies, one after the other. She then ran her hand over Nohea's ass and then between her legs again. She felt the moisture between Nohea's legs glaze her fingers.

"Taste her", she said to Kai.

Kai licked out her tongue as Yani ran her fingers over her lips, she licked and savored every drop. Nohea looked at Everett. Yani grabbed both of the girls and walked them over to Everett. She had Kai kneel before him as she sat beside him, she told Nohea to get on her kneels as well. Yani looked at Everett and they engaged in a kiss. Kai place her hand on Everett's dick and barley had full grip of it. She then took her tongue and made contact, she slid it down the base. Nohea had Yani open up her legs wider so she could get a look at her precious flower, while she rubbed on her own pussy.

Everett reached over and pulled the flower from Yani's hair letting her locs fall past her shoulders; he grasped her cheeks and pulling her in for another deep kiss. Nohea sucked at Yani's petals searching for her sweet nectar as Kai suckled at Everett's sweet stick. Yani motioned Nohea to her feet; she grabbed her hand and directed her to climb on top to find her face. As Nohea found her seat on Yani's plush lips and no longer pillows, she marveled. She couldn't help but to force feed Yani her precious plate, her body gained a mind of it's on. Yani moaned and groaned. Everett had by then laid Kai flat on back as he laid to the side as he snacked on his dish. She couldn't contain the sounds that escaped her lips so she muzzled them with a spare pillow. Everett's tongue zigged and zagged between her pink folds.

Yani slapped and grabbed at the ass of Nohea leaving marks of pleasure all around it as she surfed up and down her face. Yani's legs were gapped open as she fed on Nohea, so Everett told Kai to taste his wife. Kai rose to her knees and crawled over to Yani and licked at her soaked lips.

Kai moaned and pushed Yani's legs apart even more so that she and Everett both could tongue tackle her brazen skin.

Everett and Kai ate away at Yani, they smacked and moaned loudly as Yani squirmed. Nohea walks over to them and straddles Everett's back she kissed and rubbed it while playing with Kai's ass. She then lifted herself up over his head and began to kiss Yani and strok her nipples. Yani could feel herself begin to crack from pressure; it wouldn't be long as heat coursed through her body. She was in ecstasy, as everyone enjoyed her essence. Especially Kai, she seemed to be enjoying this meal more than Everett, as they battled for Yani's nectar. Everett began to growl; Kai moaned and picked up the pace of her tongue strokes. Yani began to grab for anything as the two competed. Everett slide his palms under Yani's ass, he had enough of this, this was all his. So he lifted his wife in the air and plunged his tongue inside of her.

Shocked the two women just watched this God-like lover devour his wife.

"Oh my fuckin goodness. Everett!" Yani yelled.

She began to cry from pleasure as she shook on her beast's shoulders. She exploded; her small frame fell on his face then he sat her down. Her legs felt like jello. The other women looked at him biting their lips as his body glowed with sweat. They both crawled over to him they looked at his solid member, each took a side as he pushed their heads into the side of his shaft, then thrusted his hips back and forth between their lips. Yani gained her strength back, climb down and took the front of the train. They sucked in unison, Everett stood over these beautiful faces, catching Yani's eyes as she looked up he felt human again. She pushed him back to a sitting position, and took his balls in her mouth and slurped like he was going to melt; the other girls took the shaft and head.

"Fuck, ride this dick", Everett groaned.

Yani stood up, stood over him and dropped down to his awaiting member. Slowly he entered her warm insides, they both exhaled. Yani rocked her hips back and forth, her muscles tightened around his dick. Everett grunted and looked up at his wife, his eyes glazed with love. She rocked faster and fucked Everett into submission. He couldn't help but fall under her trance as she never lost eye contact with him. But he felt himself slip away he fucked back. They traded blows like prize fighters. They fucked so hard and so passionate they forgot about their company, although Kai and Nohea didn't care they were got a show.

Yani knew what would get him though. She reversed her position giving Everett her back. Her tattooed frame gleaned with sweat, the dimples above her ass exposed in the light, the view alone had Everett weak. She began bounce her ass, she smacked away his hands as he tried to grip her waist. She flipped her locs around one shoulder and looked over the other it exposed her full back and neck. She could feel Everett tense up and release his warm cum inside her.

Yani got up and looked over at Kai, "Come here, I want you to clean me off of Everett's dick".

Nohea looked sad, "What about me?"

"You can sample my dish", Yani said as she smirked, Nohea was more than happy to clean her up.

The two were so into it they just wanted to relish in the couples moment. Kai wanted Everett really bad as she sucked his dick and balls and rubbed his chest. She wanted to fuck him; she wanted to feel what Yani felt.

Kai looked at Everett, his head was tilted back and his eyes closed, she stood up and slowly eased herself onto him. His thick manhood pried her open as she let out a seductive gasp. Kai slowly swayed her hips back and forth on top of Everett.

Everett was dazed and confused, he knew what he was doing but he didn't want to stop. He had never penetrated anyone but Yani since they got together in college, but it was something about Kai, so much that he needed to see what she felt like

Everett looked at Kai; his hands gripped her waist as he inhaled her scent. Her bronze skin gleamed with satisfaction. Nohea was still feasted on Yani. Yani's eyes were closed; she enjoyed the flicker of Nohea's tongue as she sucked up all her juices. She had no idea that Everett had taken possession of Kai's precious pearl. Nohea pinned Yani's legs behind her head as she sucked on her tender spots, just as Yani hands begin to roam through Nohea's hair and pushed her head deeper into her.

Kai felt all the intensity and passion that Yani felt as Everett stroked her insides. Everett was the perfect lover; he knew the exact areas he needed to touch with just the right amount of pressure to make his partner fall deeper for him. Kai was mesmerized, she leaned in kissing Everett. Everett pulled at her long black hair, running his fingers through it. Kai was nearing her breaking point just when she was snatched off of Everett.

"What the fuck you think you're doing?" Asked Yani, looking at Everett.

"What's wrong?" Said Kai.

"You are not to fuck my husband!"

"Get out", she told the girls.

The girls were shocked they thought everything was going great.

"What did I do?" Kai asked lost as to what just happened.

"Shut the fuck up and get out now!" Yani screamed.

"Baby, let me explain", Everett said nervously.

"Explain what, how you had your dick inside her? Did you like it? What the fuck did we agree about Everett?" Answer me said Yani.

"I…can't…I", Everett stuttered.

Everett was nervous; he stumbled all over his words. He tried to explain to Yani that it was an accident, that he didn't think he was just still caught up in the moment. Yani looked at him with pure disgust.

"When we chose this lifestyle we made an agreement. You knew what you were never to do, including putting your dick in some chick or being with another person alone. That's it Everett plain and simple. What were you thinking?" Yani said angrily.

The girls had grabbed their belongings and ran out in confusion. Everett got dressed while asking himself how he could be so stupid. Yani slipped back on her dress and ran out to the beach.

Everett chased after Yani his heart thumped almost cracking his chest, what the hell was he thinking. He saw her in the moonlight at the beach. He thought how could he hurt this woman after all they've been through?

"Baby listen let me explain", Everett said walking up behind Yani.

"Was it good Everett? Huh? How does your dick feel? Why would you do this to me, we made a fucking promise", Yani said glaring at Everett her eyes filled with tears, Everett hung his head in shame, "Answer me dammit!"

"Why Everett, why?" Yani said, her eyes wet looking at Everett.

He dropped his head again, "I'm sorry baby let me fix it."

"How Everett, how can you fix you dick from being inside someone?"

"Yani be logical", Everett stated.

"Fuck you and your logic!"Yani snapped.

"What you want me to do, it happened, all I can do is move forward and do the right thing from now on"

"How would you feel Everett if I went against what we promised and fucked someone else?"

"I would be hurt; it was a mistake, a stupid one. I betrayed us, what can I do?"

"You can find your own way back to the resort, that's what the fuck you can do!" Yani said walking off.

Everett ran after Yani trying not to cause a scene, "Baby just stop for a minute."

"Don't touch me, just let me think" Yani said sternly.

Everett finally convinced Yani to get in the car with him and leave, the drive back to the resort was silent.

Going Back To Cali

They next day the sun warmed Yani's face and woke her up, she reached over to Everett's spot but he wasn't there. She remembered he slept on the couch due to the fight they had. She missed him; it was one of the first nights he didn't sleep beside her that wasn't work related. She rose from the bed, her nipples stiff as they always were in the morning. She walked over to the middle of the floor and began stretching, it calmed her. Everett walked in and asked if they could talk over breakfast. Feeling more centered Yani felt it would be a good idea to talk. She walked into the kitchen and sat at the bar. Everett placed a plate in front of her and sat on the countertop across from her.

"Listen Yani, I know last night was horrible and it didn't go as planned. I made a big mistake and I know it's going to take a lifetime to fix. I caused pain to the one person that's only brought me joy. I understand if you don't forgive me, hell I don't forgive myself, but I'm sorry", Everett said.

Everett hopped off the counter and walked towards the room before Yani stopped him.

"Everett, I love you, but it hurt me to see you inside someone else. I know it was a mistake, but it's going to take some time for me to forgive you. Never do that shit again, Never!" Yani said in a broken voice.

Yani rose to meet Everett with a hug, his arms inhaled her small flesh. Her breathing loosened as her heartbeat increased. Their blood warmed, Everett kissed her forehead. He gazed into Yani's walnut sized eyes lost. Her lips were full and pouty. Everett leaned in for a kiss, Yani shied away.

"It's not going to be that easy", Yani snarled knowing she yearned for his kiss.

"Baby we should go take a shower we have to get going soon", Everett said thinking quickly on his feet.

Yani followed Everett to the shower, she saw that he was solid and knew he needed his wood chopped, she entered the shower first. Everett looked down at her ass, "My God this woman!" he thought. She grabbed her loofah and lathered it up before Everett took it from her stating that he had her covered. He placed a layer of suds on her frame he tickled at her nipples as he washed her, the front his manhood poked her back.

Yani moaned she loved when he bathed her. His large hands reached between her legs cleaning her flower being careful of her petals. Her head leaned back, mouth opened. She was now the insect in his web. He told her to bend over so he could wash her back. She obeyed; his thickened flesh now

69

toyed at the entrance of her yoni as the water splashed against them. Slowly he worked his way through the folds of her lips.

Everett dug deep inside of her, Yani gave out a yelp. Everett was in her stomach twisting her locs into his clutches and fucked her like it was their last time. She nutted and begged for him to quit but the need to let her know she was all he desired burned in him, so he fucked harder. The clapping of Yani's ass on his thigh was musical. She yelled, "Baby please", he yelled, "Take this dick". Everett threw all of himself into her, Yani cried and pleaded for mercy but it was too late Everett was on a mission. She wanted to collapse but he had her is his clutches.

Finally the climax came, he roared, "I love you. You're the best Yani, no one else".

Yani moaned back, "Whose dick is it?"

"Yours", he groaned back.

"You're not going to give my dick to anyone else right?" Yani says moaning.

"No baby I promise, I promise, It's all yours. Nobody else will ever get it", and with one last thrust Everett came, filling Yani to the brim.

Yani collapsed, Everett's stroke had done its job, he picked her up and carried her to the bed laying her down while he cleaned up and packed their things. He woke her to get dressed then they left for the airport. Yani threw on her shades, some sweats and a t-shirt. Everett carried their bags to the terminal and they awaited their flight.

She snuggled into his V-neck shirt still tired from the morning escapades. Their flight was called and they boarded the plane. They took their seats in first class and ordered drinks because neither one them liked flying so it was always difficult. It was a five and a half hour trip so they needed something to relax themselves. Yani grabbed a blanket and snuggled up against Everett. The flight took off and back to good old California they were headed. Everett dozed off and thought of the trip, all their escapades loomed in his mind, the random sex, the other partners, the beautiful memories. He thought so much he could still feel this tingling in his loins.

He woke to find Yani's mouth covering his member under the blanket, Everett's eyes rolled back into his head. "Fuck" he thought to himself. Her mouth was so warm, her tongue smooth, he could feel the back of her throat. His legs tightened, he could feel himself on the brink as she didn't stop. Everett couldn't take it and he filled Yani's mouth with his warm liquid. Yani swallowed then went back to sleep. Everett passed out not too long after.

"We will be arriving in Los Angeles shortly, please fasten your seat belts and prepare for landing", the overhead voice stated.

Yani moaned while yawning, Everett fastened their seat belts as they prepared to land. The flight went smooth they were both unconscious for most of the trip anyway, so it wouldn't have mattered if it wasn't. They exited the plane and headed for the terminal.

When they arrived at the terminal, Everett grabbed the bulk of their luggage, "So that's all you're going to take", Everett joked knowing he was more than capable of handling the load.

"Aint that what you're here for", Yani said slickly.

"There's that country girl coming out of you again, the Southern Bell of Beverly Hills, Pattie LaBelle would be proud of you", Everett joked.

"You better shut up before you sleep on the couch again", Yani jabs back.

Everett paused his stride, "Now why would you go there?"

"Why wouldn't I?" Yani questioned.

Everett nods, "You got a point there".

"So, you mad?" Yani says taking a jolt at Everett's pride.

"You about to be carrying your own shit, you better tighten up", Everett replied.

"You don't even believe that yourself", Yani smirks and walks to the car with Everett staring at her rear.

Yani hops her petite frame in the truck while Everett throws in the bags. After securing their seatbelts they drive off for the coastline.

"Sometimes I forget how beautiful it is out here", Yani says looking out the window.

"Yeah I know, it's too bad the dirty south doesn't have scenery like this", Everett continued his thrashing of her southern home.

Yani sneers, "Keep on talking and I'm going to tell my mother you don't like her cooking".

"Why you gotta bring Ms. Diane into this, you are so petty", Everett says ceasing fire.

"You are just mad because your mom loves me and you could never use those tactics", Yani giggled.

Everett tries think of a comeback, "Yeah, that's because I told her to be nice".

"Negro please. Your mom called me her daughter in law before we were even hitched, I mean married. You better not say shit", Yani says folding her arms.

"Aww baby, if you want, we can go stay on a farm with the hens and the chickens, if it will make you feel at home", Everett laughed.

Yani unfolds her arms, "You can go stay there your damn self, smart ass. I'm going to take another nap wake me up when you stop playing".

Everett threw on some subtle music and continued the ride in silence. Yani curled up in her seat and grabbed for Everett's arm to hold onto. They pulled into the driveway half an hour later. Everett got out the car and waved to one of their neighbors as he cut his yard on his riding lawnmower. Everett opened the door for Yani to get to get out.

Yani threw out her arms, "Carry me".

Everett laughed but knew she was serious, "Are your feet broken?"

"Yes", Yani said her face wearing a frown.

Everett grinned, "Aww, sounds like a personal problem".

"Everett", Yani whimpered.

"You are so spoiled, come on", Everett lifted his wife and carried her inside.

He then came back for their bags and checked the mail. In it was a letter from his mom.

She still wrote him letters even though he wasn't in school anymore.

Dear son,

Just wanted to see how you and Giyani were doing, I would have called, but I got a new phone and I don't know how to work this contraption. Your aunt sent me a text and it took an hour to find someone to read it for me and all she said was hey. Anyway, I know the season will be starting soon; I want to wish you luck, your father would be proud. Kiss my favorite girl for me.

Love Mommy

Everett walked in the house and saw Yani rubbing her stomach, "I got a letter from my mom, see, she likes me more, she didn't even mention you".

"Let me see", Yani said.

"Nope, it's private", Everett laughed.

Yani got up and stood on the couch, "Don't make me take it".

"Take it? What are you the big dawg on the yard?" Everett joked.

"What does that mean?" Yani stares in confusion.

"It's a prison reference baby, keep up", Everett teases.

"Oh, I forgot you're straight out of Compton", Yani says throwing up gang signs.

"It's outta, but you'd make a cute thug", Everett mocked.

Yani flopped back down on the couch and pouts, "Let me see it Everett".

"See what? You are so nasty, I'm about to write your mom and tell her, Dear Ms. Diane", Everett starts.

Yani takes off towards Everett, catching him in the hallway, "See track is still paying off. Now give me the letter".

Everett raised his hands as Yani held his member hostage in her grasp, "Okay, okay".

Yani started reading the letter, "You are such a liar".

Yani folded the letter and gave it back to Everett to put away. She ordered them take out. She was craving Lo Mein and knew Everett wouldn't mind having an eggroll. Everett flopped down on the couch with a beer and took off his shirt wearing just his tank top. Yani returned from upstairs wearing one of his jerseys.

"Damn, that looks good on you", Everett said taking another sip of his beer.

"Thank you baby", Yani gives him a kiss and looks for a movie for them to watch.

"What do you want to see baby?" Yani bends searching through movies.

Everett bit his lip as he caught a glimpse of her pantiless frame, "The view is great already".

"You are so nasty", Yani laughed and picked a movie.

After a short time the food arrives. They sat down on the couch and began eating, "Gosh I'm starving", Yani stateed.

Everett laughed at his wife, "I see, don't make a mess, now".

"You, shut up!" Yani snapped.

"So you want me to do the fortune cookie this time?" Everett asked.

Yani nods her mouth still full.

Everett cracked the cookie and began to read, "*If you have something dear in your life, don't let it go*".

Yani nods in agreement as they finish their food, she turned off the movie *Harlem Nights* which was one of her favorites and they made their journey up the stairs. Their long day had finally come to an end. The couple snuggled up and drifted off to sleep.

Yani greeted the morning with a smile as she woke in her bed, her black sheets embraced her tone. Last night was blissful; they slept in each other's grasp once they arrived from the airport. She missed the nights they just slept. She missed how he embraced her while the movies watched their love from the TV. Everett emerged from the shower; he walked over to his queen and blessed his lips with hers.

"Good morning to the sun...oh and that bright thing in the sky as well", Everett said as he kissed Yani's shoulder; she was his sun, all the light he needed.

She loved it when he was sweet it made her tingle, "You better stop, before you're late for work."

Everett pulled back the covers until he reached her calves, "I love your tone, the melanin of a Goddess, a body with more veracity than the ocean, a potent brain that could battle Socrates and you belong to me and I to you, do you think we can make it pass beautiful?"

With that Yani's legs spread for Everett as his kisses of poetry did their job, she loved when he was sensual. It was how he won her time in the first place. A poetry night that he wasn't supposed to be at, the same one she wasn't going to go to. But after being dragged by her friends to go and after he was convinced that it was ok to be a gentle giant, fate set in motion the setting for true love to occur...

"Guys I really don't want to be here I need to study and I also have track practice in the morning", Yani tells her friends.

"We're already here Yani just make the best of it, you never know, you might enjoy it", One of the girls chimed in.

"Half of this stuff I just don't get, I mean I've never been touched by poetry, so I don't see it the way you do", Yani stood up to leave when she saw him.

Everett rose to the stage, Yani was captured by this tall black man that looked like he could break the mic in his grasp, but he gently stroked it with soft deep words.

"Can I love you? Seriously, can I be your everything? Well honestly just a little more than something or someone...I've been there before and uh, it just doesn't feel right...At night I just want to have your thoughts in a choke hold...Not violently, silently taking over your mental magic until you visually lay me next to you telling me your secrets and jokes...That laugh you give, I've been touched by an angel but not Goddess the modest

relationships, situationships have left bad tastes on my tongue looking for more seasoning...you know like falling with a wintered heart but springing up when you warmed my beat box with your summer breeze...But those are seasons and I'm rambling trying to actually find the words I'm looking for...I think of you...No wait...I spiritually can't be without you...no not in the religious sense just common sense...Well I've never been rich but hopefully that will be my past tense...meant to socially be acceptable that we make these unforgettable post about our choice to share time...but in all honesty F their social wants I mean excuse my choice of letters in the alphabet but I only want U...C there I go again can't focus look what you did to me, no not blaming or shaming you...but dear best friend how can I be chain to you and we still fly? It's kinda restricting...No not wishing to be without you but I want us to be inseparable in spirit so that your heart beats the same way without me around, I mean if you want name tags for eternity like it's our first day on the job then I'll be Bob and you

Cindy...I don't know who they are either so why are we trying to follow in their shoes...will me not calling you my girlfriend cause you blues? Or will you understand we make our own hues...the only news they need to know is that you're my everything, not that you made me a sandwich...Camped outside your heart but I can wait just answer this for me...Can I love you? Seriously, can I be your everything? "

The applause from the crowd sparked her to chime in as well as he walked over to his friends.

"E that was deep man, who ever knew the famous Cooper would have a gift like that and seems like you caught somebody's attention", one of his teammates said.

"Man stop all that, I'm just doing my thing", Everett replied.

"Whatever bruh, you didn't even want to do this in the first place old scary ass", his other teammate snapped.

"Hey, this is my roommate Giyani she was moved by your words, although she claims poetry could never touch her", Yani's roommate states.

"Camille! Really?" Yani blushes, "You're very good with words"

"Thanks, I do this all the time, I'm Everett by the way", Everett started.

"He lying ma'am , the boy aint even want to do it, *what if they don't like it, I'm too big for this, my diaper gon show*", his teammate joked.

"Bruh, shut up", Everett sneers.

"I've seen you before, you use to cheerlead right?" Everett asked.

"Yeah, I just decided I liked track better, you look different without your helmet", that was stupid Yani thought.

Everett laughed at her coy joke, "Would you mind if I called you sometime?"

Yani blushed again, "I mean that's cool"

They exchanged numbers, what seemed like a lost night for them both, started the beautiful entrance to their relationship…

Even now, years later his words made her knees weak, while he descended between her legs, her body instantly jolting as his bearded face tickled her thighs and his lips found hers. She moaned for him just the way he liked it, she gripped his ears pulling his face deeper into her as he whispered sweet nothings to her yoni. Her thighs tightened as she was preparing to give him the last bit of his breakfast. She exploded and he didn't miss a drop.

Everett returned to a standing position his beard glistened with Yani's flavor, he wiped away the remains with his forearm like a beast just finishing a meal and continued with getting dressed. He threw on his sweats and his USC collared shirt, he was the defensive coordinator for the USC Trojans, where he also attended school, he and

Yani. He grabbed his visor and shades and headed for the door. He checked his pockets and realized he forgot his keys. He sprinted back to the door and knocked for his wife.

Yani wrapped herself into the black sheets she grabbed his keys and opened the door. Everett reached for the keys but Yani pulled them away from his reach. She instructed him to step in the door, he kissed her then tried again for the keys, once again she drew them back. Everett looked confused. She told him to drop his sweats; at first he hesitated but then obeyed, he stood there his girth hung between his thighs. Yani dropped the sheet, Everett's rod jumped; Yani smirked then dropped to her knees. She engulfed his member between her lips and began sucking rapidly. Everett's head kissed the door; he then gripped a handful of her locs and moved it with the motion of her head. She twisted and sucked, Everett's knees weakened. He was ready to explode.

"You're the fucking best baby", he moaned.

Yani moaned back, and Everett obliged those moans by filling her mouth. She swallows and sucked more, Everett began to reach for anything; his legs felt as if they were going to crack. On the inside Yani laughed. She released his solid flesh that still throbbed and smirked.

"I'm sorry baby I was just trying to get it all", Yani knew what she was doing.

Everett stood stuck for a moment as Yani pulled his sweats back up while wrapping the sheets around her frame, his breathing was sporadic. She kissed him and sent him off to work.

Yani closed the door and peered at herself in the mirror while smiling, she dropped the sheets that wrapped around her curvaceous body staring at it. Yani loved being naked. She wished everyone could enjoy being naked such as she.

"You still got it" she thought to herself.

She headed to the kitchen powered up the espresso machine, and then cranked up the stereo, humming along to the tunes of *Usher*. She opened the fridge pulled out some packed fruit and started eating it. After she was done eating she walked towards the double class doors opening it and taking in the scenery. Yani loved the outdoors, the fresh breeze pushing against her skin, the calls of nature, and the beautiful colors that coated her eyes. She stood there for a while doing her regular morning stretches.

She was so limber, bending with ease. Yani owned a yoga studio in the city called Cooper Flex Studio. She taught there at least two nights a week and when she wasn't she trusted her staff with helping their clients get to where they needed to be. Yani finished up stretching headed to the shower so she could start her day. She turned on the water to preheat it, pinned her hair up and stepped in the shower.

She lathered up, letting the pulsating water from the showerhead massage her body. The water must've hit the right spot because Yani sunk into the wall beside her. Her small hands cupped her breast, and slid them across her nipples and down to her stomach; she opened her legs and let the warm water run down to her clit. She then sat down and pulled the flexible showerhead with her. She laid it in front of her so she could free her hands and it was definitely in the right place.

Yani opened her legs wider; she slid in two fingers, the water slashed at her pink folds. She slowly stroked her fingers in and out she rocked her hips with a steady motion, her moans coated the steam filled room. Her pace picked up, faster she went in and out of her wetness with one hand and grabbed her breast with the other. She pulled her fingers away and ran them along her lips as she inserted them in her mouth to taste her sweet juices. She savored the taste while she reinserted them back inside her, her body had succumb to her antics

91

as she released herself onto the shower floor. Her body shook as she erupted and the water beat at her skin.

She felt relieved once again, she stood up and grabbed the showerhead and rinsed her body off. Yani stepped out the shower, grabbed her towel and dried off. Wiping the steam from the mirror she once again smiled at herself before she walked away.

Yani headed to her closet pulled out some blue jeans and a white tank top. No matter what Yani would wear she turned heads left and right, men and women both. She threw her clothes on the bed and headed to her dresser where she pulled out her white lace panties, dropping the towel to the floor. She slid in them one leg at a time and pulled them up her thighs and over her hips. Her ass bounced as she fully wiggled herself into her panties. She sat down on the bed, grabbed her vanilla bean oil and rubbed her body down. Her body was the perfect shade to coco, and now the sweet smell of vanilla dawned every inch of her.

Yani slid into her blue jeans and you would almost think they were painted on her. Once she had on her tank top you could see her firm nipples play peek-a-boo, she didn't need a bra her breast were the perfect mouth full. She walked back to the dresser opening a chest on it and pulled out a gold locket, and put it around her neck. She also put of a pair of gold hoop earrings. Yani went into her closet slipped on a pair of white and blue wedged heels and then threw her locs in a ponytail.

Yani called the cleaning service and then requested her house be cleaned; she also called the local market and requested some items to be delivered. She was very organized and she loved having control of her household. Now that everything was in place, she grabbed her blue blazer and shades and headed out the door. She arrived at her office half an hour later, she checked with her secretary for calls and appointments that were scheduled. Yani was very good at what she did; she had helped hundreds of couples reignite the passion and fire back into their lives. She was the go to therapist in town and she took pride in her work.

She had only been in Hawaii a few days but it seemed like forever, her clients hate when she's away. They loved her hands on ability, the exchange and the way she directs the actions of the lovers. Her sessions are set up in two parts, first she gets the couples to discuss their needs/desires and the second is where they go to a room that's filled with toys and stimulants. She made her clients feel so comfortable that they have engaged in sexual acts right in front of her. Yani has always been a force to be reckoned with, she can get anyone to do anything.

Tarek and Nikki were her first couple to see. Now they've been coming to see Yani for about a year. Things haven't really gotten better but they didn't seem unhappy to her. Yani thought they just liked to fuck in front of her. Nikki was a bigger girl, but her body wasn't bad. She had the sexiest set of nipples Yani had seen other than her own. Her eyes also caught Yani's attention; she likes to stare at Yani when she rode Tarek from the back. She had a nice ass as well. Tarek was the hood type, body covered in tattoos with golds. He had a nice piece of hardware from what Yani saw and he knew how to use it to tighten Nikki's ass up. He was cocky, talking shit the whole time. They use to fuck for about half an hour, use Yani's bathroom to clean up and leave, saying see you next time.

Yani laughed, it turned her on a bit, she often threw out tips and pointers as he stroked. She even had the luxury of recording a session for them. Now her next clients took the cake. Denise and Lila they were a happy Lesbian couple with 3 beautiful girls, one from Lila's previous relationship and 2 that she birthed with Denise. They started coming to Yani when the two decided to try bringing a man into the bedroom. Everything was fine until Denise caught him drinking breast milk from Lila's nipples.

Denise was more so pissed because she liked to do it too. The babies were no longer drinking it so that wasn't an issue, but it pissed Denise off. So they went back to just them in the bedroom, it was boring, loss of passion, no love at all. That's when they found out about Yani.

"Yani we want to thank you for helping us rekindle that spark we lost, Denise has been so much more in tune with my body", Lila said playing in Denise's curls.

"So will this be our last session?" Yani says looking over her notes.

"Yes but we want to give you something for helping us", Lila says.

Yani raises an eyebrow after watching Lila's shirt come up over her head, her full breast falling from her shirt. She began sucking on Denise's neck, her hand going into Denise's sweatpants releasing a purple dildo that was part of a strap on. She then lifted Denise's shirt, Denise was small but her breast were twice her size. Lila used two hands to support and suck each one. Denise moaned, for the first time watching a session Yani could feel herself beginning to get tuned on. She told herself never to get involved at work but watching Lila soak up Denise's breast moistened her kitten.

Lila took the purple dildo and shoved it in her mouth. Saliva poured from the sides. Yani's mouth dried and she started to overflow. Lila then dropped her skirt; a piercing glowed from behind the folds of her lips. She spread her lips and sat on the dildo her piercing shone as she bounced up and down, her pretty flesh locked around the dildo as she creamed, Yani didn't know how much she could take. Her glasses fogged, nipples hardened bursting through her shirt. She was hot and bothered.

Lila looked at her frustrations motioning for Yani to come to her. Bashful, Yani's horniness subsided for the moment as the couple finished. Lila cleaned herself off the purple toy and the couple found their way into the bathroom. Yani sat there throbbing she thought to have phone sex with Everett so she gave him a call. Soon as she heard his voice her hands found their way to her clit. She massaged it to his commands. "Your pussy daddy" she moaned. Her moans grew louder as her other hand found her breast. Everett was talking that good shit. Yani was ready to explode then her heart stopped realizing her clients hadn't left. They stood there at the bathroom door watching the whole time. Yani quickly got off the phone returning to some kind of self-structure.

"Don't worry Mrs. Cooper we won't tell a soul", the two said smiling as they left her office.

Yani smirked at herself. The phone rung, it was Everett. He was calling to make sure Yani was ok. She explained to him that she had been busted by her clients and how embarrassed she was, they both laughed. Everett knew the job wasn't complete so he told her to get up and go lock the door, she obliged. When she got back to the phone she told him it was done, and the two finished what they started.

"I want you to cum for me", Everett said to her.

Yani pulled down her jeans and opened her legs and pulled her panties to the side, she exposed her wetness. She took two fingers to her delicate flower manipulated its petals. Everett listened to her moans, he told her to remove her fingers and to taste them, one finger at a time.

"How does it taste?" he asked

"Sweet" she uttered.

Yani put Everett on speakerphone, turning the volume down so that only she could hear. She wanted both hands free. Her hand made its way back between her thighs, while the other cupped her breast. Everett told her that he was began to swell and that he wished to feel her tightness surround him. Yani's pace picked up, she fingered herself faster urging Everett to talk to her dirty.

Everett's was throbbing for her, pulsating against his thigh; he could see precum wet his pants as he stroked it. He told Yani he wanted her to fuck him, he wanted to watch her ass bounce off him. Blood begin to fill Everett's manhood so much that it was pressing hard against his sweats. Wanting to relieve himself he freed his penis and stroked it as he listened to his wife playing with herself. He could hear how wet she was and he wanted them to cum together.

"I want you to cum for me baby, spread your legs wider and pat that pretty pussy" he told her.

Yani's moans became more erratic, Everett stood up so he wouldn't make too much a mess. He stood over the wastebasket, aiming his thick member down stroking away. Yani told him she was about to cum, she moaned and said "oh shit" as squirmed in her chair, and she squirted with exhaustion. Everett, moans became deep as he played with the head of his dick "fuck yes" he said as he leaked in the basket before falling back in his seat. They both said I love you and hung up the phone.

Everett pulled himself together and started going over his playbook. He went over a play his father was famous for. He would do a stunt twist with the defensive tackles and defensive ends switching positions while the cornerback blitzed. Now the key for this was to have two linebackers that could cover and Everett had that with his two star outside linebackers. The main one being his senior who was their captain a person they couldn't lose if they wanted to make it to the National Championship. Everett's father groomed him to be just that, even at his size Everett could move like he was on skates. He thought back to the late night coachings with his dad…

"That's right Cooper now the left, come on, knees up, knees up, faster!" Everett's dad coached.

"Dad do you think I'll be good enough to play in the NFL?" young Everett asked.

"You can do anything you put your mind to E, never ever forget that hard work beats out talent when talent doesn't work", Everett's dad preached as he always did, "Okay now back to work, you had a long enough break".

Everett smiled he knew his father was his everything and he instilled that hard work in him, even now he smiled at the same time he dropped a tear for his fallen hero. Robert, Everett's father was battling cancer for the second time that had spread to his liver. The doctor told him it was terminal and that there was nothing more he and his team could do. Everett was Roberts only child and the one to seem to take the news the hardest. His father was someone he tried to mimic throughout his life and pride himself being the best to make his father proud.

Introduction

Even away from each other the couple's passion thrived. Everett looked at the picture of Yani sitting on his desk. He was finally returning to normalcy. There was a time before Yani started both jobs that she would come visit him in his office and bring him a snack. He still kept the red panties that were his favorite of hers, tucked away in one of his drawers. She had shoved them in his mouth after giving him the best head he's ever had. Everett loved Yani's freaky side but it was her heart that attached him to her the most.

There was a stretch that Everett went through when his father was really sick. Everett's father groomed him to be everything that he was and for that Yani appreciated him. Everett's father was a football coach for the 49ers back when Everett was growing up. Everett wasn't the average size boy by 16 he towered over his 5'9" father at 6'3" nobody expected it seeing as his mother only was 5'2". Everett grew two more inches by the time he was a senior.

All the colleges salivated over the chance to snatch up the amazing talent, but his father sought the one thing that most of the schools didn't start with, education. Everett grew up in the rough neighborhood of Richmond, California if not for his father's job opportunity Everett might have been exposed to more violence than he did. Having one of his childhood friends get gunned down over gang violence, Everett was kept in the house.

"Cooper", his dad would yell, once he knew homework was done. The two would go out and run drills. Everett became one of the biggest recruits ever at his position. He stood 6'5 243lbs his senior year and could tackle a tank. His hits were legendary. After his father had talks with a few schools USC became the destination for young Everett and it must have been written in the stars he'd find Giyani Sims at the time a small voice, country girl out of South Carolina, she was very petite and curvy.

In her freshman year she was 5'6 113 soaking wet. But had the most amazing eyes Everett had ever seen. It was love at first sight. At first Yani was intimidated by Everett, tall, tattooed and big. But his voice soothed her as he read his poetry she couldn't keep her eyes off of him. The two hit it off slowly and saw no one else after that.

After their second year of marriage Everett left pro sports in Miami to help his mother take care of his father in his last moments. Although he could have paid for the treatment of his father, Everett's dad was no fan of modern medicine. He watched his

105

father, his hero slowly die of lung liver. But the memories he built in this time meant more than money ever could. He never grumbled about leaving the NFL and was always smart with his money thanks to his upbringing. Yani never complained and stuck by his side. She even put her dreams aside for the time being after building a few clients in Miami. Everett never felt a love like that other than the love from his mother and father. Yani was unlike any girl he ever met. Once his father passed Everett took it hard, it was the man that groomed him to be who he was, who would he turn to? Yani, just Yani and that's what Everett needed, she helped him find peace, she was there in his father's final days. She became his strength to get back out into the football world. Following in his father's footsteps and it was all set up by Yani herself. She did the research and made the calls. Once they got back on their feet her business began booming and she was so good people flew from Miami just for her treatment.

"Coach Cooper", a voice said knocking.

Everett straightened himself up and answered, "Come in".

"Coach C, this is Makani Tachino, he is a freshman walk on from Hawaii and wants to join the team", the other coach said.

"Makani? What does that mean? Me and my wife just came from Hawaii", Everett said.

"The wind", Makani said.

Everett stood up extending his hand, "Glad to meet you, let's see what you got".

They shook hands and exited to the field. For now Makani would watch from the sideline and study along with Everett, it wasn't going to be an easy task; the process was grueling even for a freshman with his size college ball was no joke. After practice Makani introduced himself to the defense, he was humble and hungry Everett could see it, he gave him a playbook to study and told him to bring his A game to the next practice. Everett ended his day around 8, then flew home to his awaiting wife. He walked through the door and there she sat in his jersey, her leg cocked up on one side of the chair the other rested on the floor. The aroma of her essence lifted from between her panty-less thighs striking Everett's nose. Everett began walking towards her; she stops him placing her palm in the air. Everett obeyed.

She licked two fingers as she inserted them in her while she looked at Everett; he bit his lip in hunger. He began to once again move forward she stopped him, waving her finger side to side. She stroked at her lips, her wetness echoed off the walls of the noiseless house, Everett gulped. She moved rapidly her sweet sounds made him grasp at his dick. Yani stops him waving her fingers once again instructing him to halt. She then went back to work making a mess. Everett burned with want; he didn't know how much more he could take.

Yani began to splash, her liquid leaking everywhere it took everything in Everett to hold himself back. Once she was done she licked one finger then instructed Everett to come to her slowly. He obliged, she placed her moist fingers between his lips. As he suckled, she massaged his dick through his sweats, Everett grunted. She then forcefully shoved his face between her thighs. He ate like he had never had a meal before. She spilled onto his tongue. Her hands found their way to her pierced nipples; she squeezed and tugged at them.

Her back arched as she exploded on Everett's face but his fill was far from reached. He paused to rip his shirt from his body then dove back in, Yani moaned from delight she knew just what she had done, awakened her beast. Everett ate away at her soul, she cooed as his tongue stroke became unbearable. Her legs locked up as she exploded over his face, but he didn't stop. She could have drowned him for that night as far as he was concerned.

Her nails bore into his skin; her cries for mercy could be heard throughout the house. He sucked on her clit, licked her lips into convulsions, he opened his mouth wrapping his lips around her entire pussy. He spread her lips with his wide tongue. His mouth had become attached to her spout, he wanted ever single drop she possessed. She bucked uncontrollably; her chest was on fire, her eyes rolled back.

"Fuuuuuuuuuuuuuck, Everett! I...I can't take it, no more", she pleaded

Everett went deaf as her thighs had now begun to make a python like grip around his neck, his tongue speed increased, his suction took in more flesh, he slurped, the sounds kissing her ear and with one last push she was through. Her body lay limp, between her thighs throbbed, her heart rate uncontrollable. She was delusional. Everett had won the game she started. He let her lay there in her puddle to gather herself. Her king showed he was a true champion. Everett cleaned up and carried her upstairs to shower so they could head to bed.

Yani laid there, staring at her king, the sun barley peeking through the blinds. She was up early, well rested from her night of love making and eager to start her day she had a yoga class to teach and then lunch with an old friend, she just couldn't sleep anymore. This will be the first class she will get to teach since being back in town from her eventful vacation. She loved being a yoga instructor just as much as she loved being a therapist; each job had its own unique interaction with her clients. Yani has never fooled around in her studio, even though she has been tempted many times.

She crawled out of bed, being extra quiet so that she wouldn't awake Everett. Walking over to the glass doors, she opened them, taking in the morning sun. The rays kissed her body with ease as she stretched her naked frame in its light. She walked out to the balcony overlooking her backyard; she stood there for a moment smiling in elation. Yani was a happy free spirit and she lived by her own code. She heard Everett calling out for her, so she went back inside to check on him.

"Good morning beautiful", he said to her smiling.

"Good morning baby", she replied walking over to him and placing a kiss on his forehead.

"You're up early", Everett groaned.

"I see you are too", Yani Smirked.

"You so nasty", Everett said in a joking voice.

"As nasty as you want me to be", she replied.

"Oh Imma see how nasty you are Ms. Jackson, I mean Mrs. Cooper", Everett said smiling.

Yani headed to the bathroom to brush her teeth and to shower. Everett was still in bed, he watched as she stepped into the shower surrounded by clear glass. He watched as the water hit every inch of her body making it glisten. He surveyed as she lathered herself up, running her hands across her breast, till they reached her thighs. Yani's body was covered in white suds, with bubbles bursting all over her. Everett began to thicken under the sheets as he laid still gazing at her. He placed his right hand beneath the sheets and started to stroke his girth staring at her.

He wanted to join but he loved the view too much to even leave the bed. He stroked himself harder as the water hit her body to rinse the lather away. He could feel himself nearing explosion the more he envisioned being inside her. Everett pulled back the sheets forcefully stroking away until he felt the tingling sensation to release and as Yani shower came to an end he came to his vision relieving himself on his abdomen. He pulled a napkin from the night stand and wiped himself clean.

He pried himself out of the bed; he stretched as he stood to his feet still not taking his eyes off his beautiful wife as she dried herself from the distance. When she was finally dry, she slipped on her white satin robe and headed to the kitchen to cook them up some breakfast. Everett hopped in the shower to get himself ready for practice. After he showered and got dressed he met with Yani in the kitchen. She already had his coffee and food ready for him to sit down.

She turned the TV to EPSN as she did every time they had breakfast together. Everett had a game coming up soon so he had to hurry to the field to get his athletes ready because the new season was just around the corner. After breakfast Yani saw Everett out the door and on his way. She then cleaned the kitchen and got herself ready and headed to the studio.

Yani arrived a Cooper Flex Studio or CFS about an hour later. She greeted her staff and they greeted her back. She was asked questions about her vacation and she gave as much as information as she possibly could. Her staff loved her, and her free spirit. Her clients started coming in and quickly her class filled up. She had a few new faces that she had to acquaint herself with, about two young ladies and one male.

She introduced herself and got to know each one individually. She welcomed them to the studio with open arms. The male's name was Aaron Webber and she caught him staring at her quite a few times. Aaron was a handsome man, very tall and muscular. He was clean cut and clean shaven. He had a triathlon coming up so he joined the studio to get his joints loosened up. Yani's studio is next to a gym so it's not uncommon for people to come from the gym to her establishment for an added boost to their workout.

"How often do you teach?" Aaron asked.

"Only on weekends because my career takes precedent over my passion", Yani explained.

"I know what you mean I'm a lawyer", Aaron stated.

"Yeah, it's hard to find time for your passion with work always getting in the way", Yani added.

"Cool, well one of these days you're going to have to show me what you do...well, tell me. I love the studio by the way, it's really inviting goes along with the owners smile", Araon laughed.

Yani chuckled, "Will you be in class tomorrow?"

"If you're going to be here I will as well", Aaron joked.

After class ended Yani always offered fresh smoothies and refreshments to her clients free of charge. I think that's one of the reasons everyone wanted to join her studio, she just took care of you and treated you like she's known you forever.

Yani gathered her things and left the studio to go meet with her friend for lunch. Since it was a lovely day and she was only going a few blocks down the strip Yani decided to walk. Her locs laid freely down her back and a smile lit up her face, as the rays of the sun danced along her frame while she strutted down the street. She came to the small sandwich shop, where her friend Lisa was waiting for her.

Yani had known Lisa for a couple years. Lisa owned a shop for natural locs and styles. Yani had been going to her since she started on her natural journey and along the way they've grown close. Lisa was a natural beauty, with a full blown curly fro. She never wore make up, just glossed up her full lips from time to time. She also loved to wear all white as well, she thought of it as a sign of purity.

Yani walked up to the table and Lisa welcomed her with a tight squeeze. Lisa took the liberty of ordering herself and Yani a green tea and some honey butter croissants. Yani was very attracted to Lisa, but she never acted on her attraction. She enjoyed their time spent every Saturday afternoon.

"So girl how was your trip?" Lisa asked.

"It went well for the most part, very much needed. You should go", Yani said.

"Girl I see the new ink, I'm scared of needles though", she said laughing.

"Yeah the guy was dope, I felt it was time to take ahold of my past", Yani said proudly.

"Anything crazy happen?" Lisa asked.

Yani gulped, "No girl why you say that"

"You know, a couple on an Island ya'll aint make a Ray J and Kim K video?" Lisa joked

"Nah we just enjoyed each other", Yani said deflecting the question.

They ordered food and talked a little more, as they laughed and caught up. Lisa was in a relationship and wanted to know how to spice it up a little more so she asked Yani for suggestions. Yani suggested that they go to a sex shop, to see what she could find that Lisa would be comfortable with introducing in the bedroom. Once they finished up their lunch and paid they got up and walked back to Yani's car so they could go see what they could find.

Yani and Lisa arrived at the shop a few minutes later. Once inside the clerk asked to see their ID, Lisa laugh.

"What, do you think we're teenagers?" Lisa said to the clerk.

"No! But you're not far from it!" he said back to them with a smirk on his face.

They entered the other part of the shop where all the adult material was. Yani walked over the leather whips, running her hand down the stick smiling at Lisa. Lisa blushed. She was amused by all the different shapes and sizes of dildos on the wall. She's never even so much as used a vibrator. Lisa's body was super thick; she had a pear shape with light skin that was enhanced by freckles that were perfectly placed. Her white sundress hugged every curve of her with ease, and that one dimple on the right side of her face sunk deeply when a smile graced it.

Lisa stared at Yani as she thumbed through the store. Lisa had a secret crush on her. She watched as Yani passed the full length mirror watching her ass bounce as she walked in her yoga pants, and her breast nicely raised in her tank top. Yani's nipples pierced through her top slightly from the chilled air in the store. Yani could feel Lisa eyeing her; she could feel the energy around her. As Lisa passed Yani, she got a quick feel of her plump ass. Lisa wanted her, she was tempted to grab a hand full of her ass but she just kept walking.

"Watch that big ole thing", Yani smirked.

Yani called Lisa over to the lingerie section. She showed Lisa a red sexy baby doll teddy, Lisa blushed a little.

"You think that would look good on me?" she asked Yani.

"Hell yeah, have you seen your body? And you're always in white so when you break out in this red hot number anyone would be ready to fuck you senseless. I know would", She told Lisa.

"What was that?" Lisa asked.

"Nothing, try it on", Yani requested.

Lisa went to the dressing room to change. When she came out Yani couldn't believe how stunning she was. Lisa admired her own body in the mirror, smiling from ear to ear.

"Turn around", Yani told her.

Lisa turned around slowly, facing Yani. You could see straight through the teddy. Yani was

121

shocked to see that both nipples were pierced, she smiled in amazement. Her breasts were perfect.

Yani began to bite her lower lip unconsciously, "Wait, I thought you didn't like needles. Damn you look good though...I mean your dude is going to love that".

Lisa noticed it and it excited her, "Girl, I said I was scared of tattoo needles, the piercing was heavenly though and what dude?"

Before Yani could respond Lisa walked up and kissed her on the lips. Yani stood there in shock for a second and then started kissing her back. Lisa pushed Yani in the dressing room, Yani still in shock but compliant. She thought about Everett for a second but Lisa was so persistent. Lisa felt Yani's pussy through her yoga pants, but it was too much fabric to get the feel she was looking for. Lisa then put her hands inside Yani's panties and felt the warm and moist areas of her. Yani began to pant, trying to resist getting any deeper. Lisa pulled on her shirt and started sucking on her breast skillfully pulling on her nipples with her teeth, while her fingers were still inside Yani's blossoming flower.

Lisa could feel Yani get wetter and wetter. She stroked her insides faster and faster until Yani juices started running down her forearm.

Knock! Knock!

"You guys ok in there?" asked the store clerk.

"Yes", Lisa replied pulling her hand out of Yani's pants.

"Let me know if you need anything", he shouted back.

Yani couldn't believe she let Lisa have her way with her. She gathered herself, shyly looking at Lisa as she changed back into her white sundress. Lisa grabbed the red teddy and told Yani she thinks she's found what she was looking for. They left the dressing room and paid for the lingerie and left then shop.

It was a quite ride back to Lisa's shop; Yani was a bit confused since she is use to being in control. Here she was holding back her attraction to Lisa just to have the tables turned on her. The only person she's let have their way with her without question has always been Everett, well that is until today.

Lisa shop was closed for day but Yani still needed her hair redone. Lisa unlocked the doors and walked in with Yani. Lisa's shop was nicely decorated with black art and greenery. Yani took the first seat under the shampoo bowl. Lisa turned on some music and then the water. Yani relaxed as Lisa ran her smooth fingers through her locs. She massaged her scalp; Yani closed her eyes in bliss.

"Damn that feels good", Yani moaned.

"Keep talking like that and I'm going to have you wanting to marry me", Lisa joked.

Yani giggled, "You so crazy, but those hands are magical".

Lisa thought for a moment and stated, "About earlier I wanted to experience your touch I'm glad you allowed me to".

"You gave me no choice, I'm going to have to pay back your aggression one day though", Yani retorted.

"All that talk of my ass, I had a gut feeling you'd go for it", Lisa slyly replied.

"Mm hmm, you keep on with those hands and that next time will be real soon. But for now I'm just going enjoy this life you giving to my hair right now, mmm to the left a little please", Yani stated blissfully.

Yani just closed her eyes and drifted as Lisa worked wonders on her hair. She did think back to the moments where she felt controlled by this vixen.

Yani wanted to have her hands on her again, but she wanted more than just a hair massage.

Everybody Wins!

"In here baby", Everett yelled.

Everett stood over the stove in his suck the cook apron and socks. Yani smiled as a bushel of roses lay on the counter with a note on it. Through her busy week she forgot about her birthday. The fresh rosemary and seasoning filled her nose. She gazed over Everett's naked back her name shined brightly at the bottom of his neck. She loved when he cooked, Yani learned a great deal about Everett when they got together. He loved to cook. He spent a lot of time with his great grandmother, she owned a restaurant and he spent a lot of summers working part time with her.

Luckily Yani was able to meet her before she passed away. Her favorite meal that she cooked was shrimp, sausage and steak gumbo. It wasn't the most romantic meal, but it touched Yani's heart in a way that filet mignon couldn't. She removed her coat and sat at a table where a freshly poured glass of wine and fresh cut starwberrries sat awaiting her. Her thick lips compressed on the fruit, falling down the front of her bottom lip touching her chin before she caught the juices.

"Making a mess I see", Everett said smirking.

Laughing, she sipped the wine as he placed the plate before her; he then pressed his lips against hers. Then he sat down asking her "how did I do?" They laughed as she made a comment about how he still had work to do even though she wouldn't stop eating. Yani cleaned her plate to Everett's delight.

"Damn baby, big mama would be proud of you. You put those big ass feet in there", Yani said patting her stomach.

Everett grinned showing his whites and chuckled, "Ready for dessert?"

"I can't eat another..." Yani started before being stopped.

"My dear beautiful wife, don't be selfish, the dessert is not for you, come here", Everett said as he placed a can of whipped cream and strawberries on the table.

Yani smirked and stood up, "Hmm, only if you had some chocolate".

Everett smirked as Yani began to loosen her wrap around dress, as it opened it revealed a deep purple lingerie set. She walked over and stood in front of Everett. He kissed at her stomach and let her dress fall to the ground. Everett reached in his apron pulling out a blindfold. He handed Yani the mask and instructed her to put it on. She did as told; he guided her in front of him then set her onto the table. He kissed at her thighs looking up to see her bite her lips.

Everett stood up and walked towards the head of his wife. Her full lips called for him. Grabbing a strawberry he rubbed it along her lips, using it to part them before letting her bite it. He then took a pair of red cuffs and clasped her hands above her head. He slipped one of her breast from her bra and he embraced her nipple between his lips and sucked as the metal clank against his teeth. He removed his teeth from her flesh and strolled around to her thighs again. He removed her panties, her berry already dribbled with nectar. Everett salivated. Her clit thumped at him, he took his wide tongue and stroked at her clit once, then lifted his head back.

Yani's chest began to pump; her breaths grew wild, "Evere...Everett...why did you...why'd you stop?"

Everett smirked, "Hmm, not sure if I want to finish."

Yani twisted, Everett watched as her clit swelled, he toyed with her until it became unbearable to him and he engulfed her. She gasped, her back rose from the cold table. He snatched the whip cream and layered her nether skin. He licked at the sugar coating then took a strawberry and dipped it against her flesh striking her clit. She groaned as her handcuffs knocked against the table. Everett took a bite of the strawberry before sharing the remains with her. He then dove his face between her thighs covering his lower face in cream.

"Fuck yes! Eat this pussy!" Yani screamed.

Everett smacked away like his meal would melt, he didn't even come up for air. Yani squirmed, cheering on her husband. He knew it was the fourth quarter, 4th down with one play left he flickered and twirled his tongue. Her thighs tightened, it was on its way, the most explosive orgasm she has had in a while. His lips locked to her clit. He wasn't letting go. She pleaded, cried and groaned, they went unanswered. He ate away at her flesh licking from the tip of her lips down to her ass. She came; she couldn't take it anymore her body jolted before she collapsed in defeat. Everett removed his apron and wiped his face.

He steered her to the shower; he turned on the water and submerged both of their bodies in the steam. He kissed her hard, she kissed back. He gripped the back of her locs passionately. The water recoiled off their skin. She swathed her legs around his torso, then dropped herself down on his engorged manhood. Just to come back up and bite into his shoulder. He grunted throwing her against the wall, thrusting deeply inside of her. She gripped his head and looked into his eyes as he pumped away violently.

"Cum for me you want to, I know it", Yani stroked at Everett's heart with her eyes and in no time he came inside her warming her belly.

They passed out on the shower floor until the water ran cold. After drying off they cuddled into the heat of their sheets and fell asleep.

Yani kissed his arms, she pressed her back against his chest. Everett kissed the back of her head as the sun gleamed on them.

"I love you, you know that?" Everett whispered.

"How much?" Yani replied.

"I can't tell you", Everett answered.

Yani turned to Everett, "What do you mean?"

"To be honest baby there's no word that can describe it; I'll never lie to you. And I would never use a word that can't even fathom my love for you. No baby, I wouldn't disrespect you like that", Everett said as he kissed her forehead, "Now you lay there, I'm going to make breakfast".

"Everett", Yani whispered from her laying down position.

Everett turned back, "yes baby"

"I love you too", Yani replied.

After breakfast they went out to the beach to work out. Everett wasn't the most fanatic when it came to aerobics but he knew how much Yani loved yoga. They stretched on the cool beach sand; there was a unruffled breeze although the sun light covered their bodies it was cool air. Everett was still taken by Yani's figure even though he saw it every day. Her curves called for him. Everett thought about perusing poetry again and since they lived so close to the beach he had the seclusion he needed. But his passion for football outweighed it. Sometimes he'd watch as Yani stretched and did yoga and jotted down ideas. Even in the passionate midst of love making he found time to spill some words to Yani's mental.

Yani loved it, his bass beat against her body. Her frame curved to his every letter. Sometimes they'd bathe and he'd share some old work he remembered, it was just a different side of him that no one really knew, her gentle giant.

"*The sun wept only to be outshined by the star that would not go away when it rose, she was named my love and beat so radiantly she masked the wings she walked the Earth with*", Everett spoke as his thoughts came back to Yani.

"One of these days I'm going to tell the other coaches, how soft you can be. How did you say it when we first met? I do this all the time", Yani Joked.

"And one of these days you're going to need me to get something off of the shelf and I'm just going to walk away", Everett turned his back.

Yani jumped on his back as they tumbled to the sand. The thoughts of kids floated through her head, his long arms wrapped her up. They shared lip exchanges as the water kissed the beach. Once they finished it was time for Everett to get dressed for the game. Everett left for the game having to be there early as Yani stayed home to get dressed. Yani always attended, she wore her colors proud, still being able to wear her gear from freshman year, well the shirts. The pants and shorts were a no go. Her ass had escalated since then and there was no going back. Yani walked out the door and drove for the game.

Everett was one of the top defensive coaches on the west coast. He had NFL offers but loved the college atmosphere and made enough money where it wasn't an issue. Yani arrived at the stadium and made her way towards the student section. You couldn't tell who was more excited in the stands Yani or the other college kids. She was a sports fanatic, so she adored it. She had box office seats but treasured the atmosphere inside the stands.

"Hey girl", Lisa waved.

Yani forgot she invited her, "Hey there!"

They exchanged cheek kisses as Lisa sat down. Yani thought should she mention their encounter to Everett. She thought to ask Everett if she could join them, she did love her aggressive nature and after all it was her birthday still, technically. She contemplated the idea. But for now she enjoyed the game. They both leaped up as the interception by the Defense went back for a TD. By the 4th quarter the game was well in hand and they quickly finished them off. Drinks, thought Yani. Having drinks is how she would do it.

After convincing Everett to celebrate they headed home to change. Yani adorned a constricted red dress and heels to accentuate, the red bounced off her deep brown skin and hugged her every curve. Her pierced nipples pressed through the fabric of her dress so they could get some shine. Everett threw on some slacks and red fitted Polo shirt. They dressed and headed to the lounge to drink and chill with a room in VIP. Lisa was going to meet Yani there. The VIP area was at the top of the lounge, the area had a seating section equipped leather white couches with red plush pillows; two end tables accented them and held buckets of champagne, there was a little dance space right before you reached the black and red sheer curtains. Everett sat down with his favorite drink in hand, Hennessy.

The lights bounced around them, Yani looked up from her glass of Patron to see Lisa in a tight white wrap dress, her breasts were spilling out. Yani's mouth salivated. Lisa knew she was a vixen.

"So this handsome specimen is Everett? Way to go Yani!" Lisa exclaimed.

Yani never thought that they had never met, "Yep this is my baby!"

"Baby? Girl that's a man, stand up for me, Mr. Everett", Lisa joked. Everett stood up towering over Lisa, "Yeah girl I see why you got him".

138

Everett smirked and sat back down next to Yani, "Ok your turn girl let me see that dress", Lisa said.

Yani stood, "This old thing?" She replied.

"Look at all that ass", Lisa said smacking Yani on the butt catching Everett's attention.

"Girl stop all that, what you been drinking?" Yani said laughing.

"Nothing yet but I'll be right back", Lisa said leaving the area.

Yani looked at Everett this was her chance, "Listen baby a few days ago Lisa and I had a moment in the dressing room while she was getting lingerie. I'm sorry I should have told you sooner".

"What do you mean by a moment?" Everett questioned.

"Some kissing baby, I promise that was it", Yani stared into his eyes.

Everett turned his head and swallowed his pride, thinking about the backlash he took for his actions back in Hawaii. For now he would allow things to play out as he smirked, plus it was her birthday, "It's cool baby. No harm done right?"

She felt a little bad but felt he was honest about it being nothing. Lisa returned with a bartender carrying shots and an assortment of drinks. The couple smiled as they welcomed the drinks. With that the party was on. Shots were tossed back. But things got interesting when body shots came into play. Lisa untied her dress wanting to be the first, her lace bra and panties held her curves perfectly. She laid on top of the table and awaited for lips to bless her body. Everett stationed himself at her naval while Yani waited at her neck and breast area.

The couple nodded then commenced pouring the liquor onto her body, they quickly slurped it off to her delight as heard through her moans. She loved it, she gripped Yani's locs as she sucked at her neck. Then it was Everett's turn, Yani again took the upper area while Lisa got his naval. The girls nodded then poured, Yani attacked his neck, clawing at his chest, then she kissed him as his hands found her ass. Meanwhile Lisa sucked at Everett's stomach while rubbing on his manhood through his slacks. Yani raised her eyes to see the sight of Everett's enjoyment. She kissed harder as she heard him begin to moan and grunt.

Lisa kissed Everett's waistline looking up at Yani that deep dimple bore into her cheek as she smirked. Then she pecked at his dick print sucking the outline.

"Don't be scared, you can suck it if you want to", Yani states.

Shocked for a minute Lisa looked at the couple, Yani's nipple now in Everett's mouth. She looked at his zipper a moment then back at Yani who was enjoying Everett's mouth. Yani moans for her to proceed as she looked at his bulge. She exhaled and plunged herself in their world before pulling down the zipper and revealing Everett's erection. She was surprised by the thickness but let her infatuation go and stuffed him between her lips. Moans could be heard from Everett's lap, the club lights bounced through the curtains and sparkled on Lisa's freckles, her hair was pulled back into an afro puff.

Yani elevated her dress and straddled Everett's face. He smacked away as Lisa had his dick trapped between her breasts, she was sloppy, spitting and slobbering at his thick piece. Yani bounced up and down her ass pounding against Everett's chest; he reached down to grab Lisa's puff. Her head viciously bobbed loosely, he thrust up. The choking sound turned him on, he almost came.

Yani came and saturated Everett's beard, then walked up and lifted Lisa by her hair. She gripped her roughly, turning the tables from their previous encounter.

"I told you I was going to get you", Yani smirked.

Before Lisa could speak Yani kissed her, and plucked at her soaked nipples, they were softer than she remembered. Everett lay there patiently, as the two exchanged kisses and groped each other. Yani hopped on top of Everett and inserted him into her. Lisa sat on Everett face so she could see Yani's face. In unison they took turns, Lisa fucking his tongue and Yani his dick, at the same time kissing each other.

Lisa's ass was indulgent as it applauded above Everett's nose. The sweet taste of strawberries leaked from her pussy. Yani began to cream on her husband, she watched Lisa go desolate on his face. She wanted them to cum together. She kissed her and gripped her hair "cum with me", she chanted in between breaths. The splashing sounds played in their ears, Yani felt Everett's warm liquid fill her stomach. It turned her on so much that she fucked him harder, Lisa shrieked she was cumming,

Yani told her to hold on she felt fire in her. Her stomach constricted, she began shivering before leaking down Everett's shaft with her nectar. They sat there spent; Yani's eyes glowed as she got her birthday wish. Lisa found the strength to lift off Everett's face and make her way to collapse on the couch.

Yani bent down kissed Everett, "Thank you for tonight".

Everett smiled, "I love seeing you happy. I'll do whatever it takes to make that possible".

"Can y'all call me an ambulance, my goodness Everett that tongue of yours", Lisa chimed in.

Yani lifted off of Everett and went over to Lisa, "Come on girl we gotta get out of here".

The two kissed a few times before calling Everett over to share. Yani grabbed something out of her purse to clean them. They dressed and headed out the lounge, none the wiser to what had transpired. Lisa hugged and kissed the couple goodnight before she departed.

Yani and Everett hopped in the car and drove home. On the ride home Yani thanked Everett again for giving her a memorable birthday. She knew that Everett would go to the ends of the earth to satisfy her and he has never disappointed her in that aspect. It begin to rain on the way home, Yani loved the rain. Sometimes when it's late at night and raining Yani would go out on the balcony and just sit and stare at the sky, she found it to be very therapeutic. The sound of the raindrops hitting the roof, the bouncing off the leaves, and the way the water glistened on the street under the moonlight was calming to her.

Yani began taking off her dress in the car, Everett looked at her. He knew she was up to something he just didn't know what. He didn't care however he loved the way her skin shined and the sleekness of its tone. The way he looked at her was if they had just met. She loved that about him, that he can still look at her in the same light even after all these years of being together. Yani stripped down to her lingerie, she then removed her heels at the same time Everett was pulling up in the driveway of their home.

Yani jumped out the car holding her hands out by her sides. She tilted her head back, letting the raindrops hit her faces. The rain was calm and steady. She let her locs down as she began twirling around laughing. Everett smiled at the joy of his beautiful wife dancing in the rain. Everett removed his shoes and walked towards Yani. She opened her eyes just in time as he was wrapping his arms around her. Everett looked at her, cupping her face. Yani gazed at him with her big brown inviting eyes. He kissed her.

Their kiss was warm and passionate. They stood in the rain, without any worries, any cares; just love and warmth. Everett scooped Yani up and carried her drenched body to the door. He opened the door and inside they went, full of love.

They walked upstairs and to the bathroom and dried her wet body. He touched her with such tenderness, she was delicate to him. He admired the art that adorned her scars and kissed at them. He thought to himself about how much she meant to him, and that he never wanted to lose her. She looked down at him and smiled. He removed her lingerie and covered her body in a terry wrap and then carried her tired body to the bed.

They laid there listening to the raindrops hit the roof. The water covered the window and lit up the walls with shadows created by the moonlight. They snuggled not a word exchanged between them just shared spirits. She caressed his face as he stroked her back. There was a rumble that followed the flash of lightning but the two were so caught up in bliss neither budged. Everett pulled her in tight their heat now inflamed. Electrons bounced between them with enough force to create energy.

147

Everett kissed her soul and talked to her heart as they drifted off to sleep.

Full Of Surprises

Everett let Yani sleep through the morning, she awakened around eleven. She could hear Everett on the telephone in the living room as she got out of bed. She put on her robe, tied her hair up and headed to the bathroom. After she washed up and brushed her teeth she headed out to greet her husband. Everett was in the kitchen reading the paper.

"Good Morning Baby!" says Yani.

Everett turns and wraps his arms around Yani giving her a big hug.

"How did you sleep?" he asked.

"After a night like last night, I slept like a baby. Thank you once again baby, I had a great time for my birthday!" She says.

Everett smiled, his way of saying "you're welcome." Yani sat down at the nook and ate some oatmeal while Everett read the paper. After eating, Yani went off to teach her yoga class. Everett still planned to on celebrating Yani's birthday throughout the entire weekend so he called up some old friends and invited them over to the house for a barbeque. He even invited people from her yoga studio but advised them not to clue her in on what he had planned.

Everett called up one of his friends, who happened to be a chef to help pull everything together for tonight's festivities. Yani would be off teaching her class and getting her hair done, so he had time to set up and prepare everything for when she came home. Everett also called in a housekeeper to keep everything clean; he didn't want Yani to have to lift a finger this weekend unless it was to put it in his mouth.

It was nearing 5 o'clock, everything was coming together. The chef had prepared a world class menu for this old fashion style cookout. Their backyard dawned lanterns hanging from the trees, a fire pit, a huge barrel grill filled with meats and veggies. The cake had arrived and was hid in the dining area so Yani wouldn't see it till it was time. The sun was beginning to set and people had started arriving. Only thing that was missing was Everett's wife beautiful face.

Kristen, one of Yani's instructors came inside to let him know that Yani was pulling up in the drive way. Everett told everyone to take their places and to be quite. They could hear the keys jingle at the door and hear Yani fumbling around with bags.

"Surprise!!" everyone yelled when the door sprung open.

Yani's beautiful face lit up in amazement. She thought Everett was at work, but he was instead at home preparing a get together for her. Everyone walked up to Yani wishing her a happy birthday and presented her with gifts, she was almost in tears. She told everyone she would be right back she wanted to go freshen up, besides she had been working out, getting her hair done and doing a little shopping. Yani came back a half an hour later, looking stunning in a cream maxi dress.

She was just a natural beauty. Her locs were in a French braid draping down her back, her melanin glowed and her full lips gleamed. A gold locket hung from her neck and diamonds dripped from her ears. She walked outside where mostly everyone was gathered and it was as if she had just stepped onto the stage, everyone looked at her and cheered.

Yani had a prevalent smile on her face. She mingled with the crowd, making her way to speak and interact with everyone. She walked over to Kristen who is standing talking to Aaron.

"Hi", said Yani.

Both Kristen and Aaron spoke back to her.

"You look beautiful", exclaimed Aaron.

"Didn't expect you to be here, but thank you", Yani replied

"Everett called and invited everyone so Aaron and I had come to the party, he lives in my neighborhood", Kristen stated.

Yani stood there talking to them for a bit before Everett came to whisk her away. He told her how ravishing she looked and stole a kiss from her in between her words. Once she and Everett embraced she could see out her peripheral that Aaron was staring at her, she gave a slight smile before kissing her husband on the cheek.

153

Everyone was enjoying themselves, the food and the music. Yani was so happy. Everett was talking with his friend, the chef, about getting the cake ready to bring around. As the chef went off to get the cake he told Yani to come stand under the lanterns. He then stood behind her and covered her eyes pressing himself against her so she could feel his manhood. Everett then removed his hands and there before her was a 3 tier red velvet cheese cake, one of her favorites.

Yani blew out the candles. The cake was cut and Yani had a taste before dropping a little bit on her dress. She excused herself to go clean off and headed to the bathroom. Yani was in the guest bathroom with the door slightly ajar, the door crept open and it was Aaron.

"Excuse me, I'm in here", Yani grasped at her clothes.

"My apologies, but you're beautiful", Aaron smiles.

"Thank you again but you need to leave my husband does live here, with me and is here now", Yani says pointing to the door.

"It's just something about you, I really enjoy the talks we have after yoga class", Aaron says pushing up on her.

Yani's head clouds, she thought of her husband's infidelity but this wasn't the time or place, "You need to…"

Aaron grabbed her and kissed her, "I'm sorry I had to".

Yani was speechless, a little lost in the moment.

"Baby, you ok?" Everett yelled from down the hall.

Yani snapped out of it and panicked pushing Aaron out the bathroom and into the guest bedroom quickly before Everett turned the corner. Aaron stood behind the door hoping that either Everett would leave or they would leave together. The last thing he needed was for him to come into the guest bedroom. Yani was just finishing up and gathering herself before Everett walked in and closed the door. Aaron thought to stay in the bedroom but felt it was best if he joined the other guest outside.

"I want you right now", Everett said.

Everett turned Yani facing the mirror, pulled up her dress and bent her over. He then dropped to his knees spreading her cheeks. He licked at her floret, spreading each petal with his tongue. Yani tried to keep herself together, trying not to make too much noise. Everett lapped and drank and dove his tongue deep in her pussy until he knew she was at the point of orgasm. Just when her knees became shaky he stopped. He stood up and pulled out his rock hard dick.

He took no time forcing himself inside her. Yani let out a little yelp.

"Shhhh", said Everett.

Yani sealed her lips, but you can see on her face the pleasure and pain. Deeper he stroked, grabbing at her neck as she leaned into his chest. She was wet, juices drowning his dick and running down her leg. Everett groaned in her ear, nibbling on her lobe. They were almost near orgasm when there was a knock on the door. Everett didn't care about who was at the door, he was going to have his wife cream on his dick.

He fucked her harder. He stroked her deeper. He watched as her ass bounced on and off his dick. Yani legs became unsteady, she could feel his girth thumping inside her and at the last long deep thrust they came in unison. After cleaning up they left out the bathroom one at a time. Once back outside Yani thanked everyone for coming and for the gifts. The party went on for another hour or so before it started dwindling down. There were only a few people left so everyone came inside. Everyone helped clean; Yani and Everett just were surrounded by good friends. Everyone took to their kind spirits.

Kristen told Yani that she and Aaron were about to leave because she had to be at the studio early in the morning. Yani walked them both out, Aaron gawked at her the entire way. She stood at the edge of the driveway waving them off. Once she got back inside she ran to Everett jumping into his arms and thanked him for a lovely evening.

Everett playfully popped Yani's butt asking her if she wanted to watch a movie. She ignored him waiting for him to do it again. Soon as he did it the second time she turned around and grabbed his crotch. Everett threw up his hands like a guilty suspect. After all she was holding some precious equipment in her hands. They finally agreed to watch a movie, well mostly Yani's decision. The rain began knocking against the roof and porch, such a serine ending. They cuddled on the couch and put an old movie on, Love and Basketball. Yani smirked then reached for her ankle remembering her stumble but was ready to prove herself tonight.

She jumped up, Everett's eyes light up a bit startled by her actions.

"Come on chump, payback time", Yani says placing the white waste basket that sat on the side of entertainment center in front of them.

She then balled up a piece of one of the magazines that were spread across the coffee table. Everett sat flabbergasted thinking she just had too much to drink. So he sat there and just smirked.

Yani marched over and pushed him, "I said get up".

Everett smiled and got up towering over Yani, "You really want this work huh?"

"If I didn't I wouldn't have said it chump, game time", she looked up smirked and then grabbed his girth, Everett flinched and she then took the paper ball and dunked it while he was distracted.

"Umm scuse me sir, but I think you must lose some of that clothing", Yani teased.

Everett relieved his shirt. Yani smirked as he made his chest jump, "You know I love it when you do that".

Everett smiled, "Cut the talk let's do this".

Yani started to air dribble then stopped, "Ouch!"

Everett pulled up from his defensive stance, "What happened baby?"

"My nipple it hurts, I think I caught it on the fabric", Yani pouted.

Everett examined it, "Looks fine baby".

"Kiss it please", Yani pleaded.

Everett bent to kiss it, "Okay baby how about now?"

"Perfect, all better", Yani shoots the balled up paper into the basket.

"Really baby", Everett raises an eyebrow.

"All's fair, now drop them pants baby boy", Yani laughed.

Everett released the buckle on his pants and stood his boxer. He bends to play D on Yani. She backed up into his crotch then tried to spin off of him for another basket, but Everett caught her, he wrapped her up and sucked on her neck. She dropped the paper ball; Everett picked it up and dunked. Yani began to remove her dress.

"Hmm so I guess you win again", she dropped her dress to the floor.

Everett stared as the light from the TV bounces off her skin. Yani walked towards Everett her eyes low and seductive. She gets on her tip toes and wrapped her arms around his neck. She stared into his eyes and he into hers. He kissed her deeply taking one hand and clutching beneath her ass. She giggled and then moaned as she felt the heat from her pussy rise. Everett's dick stiffened, Yani's pierced nipples pushed against Everett's chest.

"Did you enjoy your day my Goddess?" Everett bellowed.

"Yes baby, I don't know how this night can get any better", Yani smiled as Everett's manhood press against her exposed parts.

Everett took Yani's hand and walked her upstairs and out the balcony doors. The rain splashed against their bodies, Yani smiled as the water kissed her skin. Everett had one more surprise. He told Yani to close her eyes, Everett sat her down on the lounger she felt the puddle of water underneath her ass. She laid back and allowed her locs to lay on her shoulders. She rubbed at her nipples the rain made her extremely horny. Everett told Yani to open her eyes, he stood there naked with the moon glow behind him and the rain bounced from his body. Yani lifted herself to bring her favorite toy to her mouth, being the pleasing person she was. But Everett stopped her and told her to lie back onto the lounger.

Everett bent and kissed her while stroking at her clit, Yani moaned into his lips as his fingers swirled faster. Yani jerked, Everett knew what time it was. He kneeled between her thighs putting as much of his body onto the lounger as possible. He began lapping at her kitten; he pushed the folds of her lips back getting to her inner pussy. She could be heard smacking against her nipples above Everett's head. Yani's back arched, her stomach warmed her chest tightened, she gripped his ears and began grinding against his face until she exploded. Everett wouldn't cease his wrath.

The water trickled down Yani's lips soothing her cries, "Please Everett, please...I can't, I can't take it".

Everett smirked he knew she was at her breaking point, so he pulled up. Yani attacked his dick and sucked away like it was the last one she'd ever have. But Everett wasn't having it, though it felt incredible he made tonight about her so he lifted her onto his lap. He slide inside of her, he gripped

163

her back as she dug into his. He growled, the rain beat against their bodies and cooled them off. Everett pumped, Yani gripped his head, her locs were wet and touched her back. They kissed passionately, then violently tearing at each other's bodies. He fucked, she fucked back. She pulled, he pulled.

The loud splashing sparks in their ears, sounds rumbling in the wet night air. It was thunderous applauding from their bodies as the climax approached. Explosions clashed as the mass of passion had reached its max. They blasted off with the veracity, the capacity level intangible to some. Only certain ones can understand this strand of love. Never bland, Everett filled Yani with every ounce of liquid inside of him. They laid for a while before going inside and drying off. Yani fell asleep in Everett's arms. They slept into the late morning.

Now What?

A few days pass, Everett and Yani separated themselves from the world. She looked at Everett and rubbed his sleeping face and caught a glimpse of the time, she realized she was late. She quickly snuck out of the bed and got dressed for work. Yani rushed out the house running late. She zoomed into her parking space and rushed inside passing her secretary who was holding a file folder. She opened the door and dropped her things on her desk. She told her secretary to send in her clients as she apologized for her tardiness she looked up and saw Aaron.

Aaron sat on the couch with his wife Sasha; they had been married for little over 5 years. They had one child together and had grown apart in the recent year. After seeking marriage counseling and not finding any help with that they decided to give it one more shot, with a few sessions with a sex therapist. Yani was shocked to see Aaron on her couch but she introduced herself as if it was the first time they have met.

She sat down and once every was formally introduced she gave them a run down on her services and how she could be an assistance to them,

Aaron and Sasha spoke candidly about their relationship. After their daughter was born two years ago everything changed. Aaron spoke of Sasha as a loving and caring wife but she just didn't have the same drive for him prior to their daughter's birth. But Sasha begged to differ. She exclaimed that being a mother and a working woman she rarely has time to do the things that they use to. Aaron tried to say it's all about balance but she just cut him off like his opinion was irrelevant.

Yani asked Sasha "What is it about Aaron that turns you on?"

Sasha paused and turned to Aaron and looked into his deep chestnut eyes.

"I love the way he looks at me. I could be in the kitchen cooking dinner and he would be sitting on the couch just staring at me. He would get up and come towards me saying little sweet nothings, it would turn me on. He would pick me up and sit me on the counter top lifting up skirt and place his hands between my thighs and then he would insert a finger. He only wanted to see how wet he had made me so he could have a taste. He would then put his finger in his mouth and tell me how he couldn't wait to eat. That turned me on!"

Yani was becoming moist. Each time Sasha spoke of him, her legs would tighten together underneath her desk. Aaron caught Yani gawking at him, he looked at her he gave a little boyish smirk.

"And Aaron, what turns you on about Sasha?"

Yani sat up in her chair, composing herself.

"Her! I love when her look is effortless. Before she relaxed her hair, she was all natural. I would just stare at her while she slept, hair all over the place, her big full lips pouting in her sleep. Her scent turned me on. I'd wait till she is in a deep sleep;I'd slowly peel back the covers so I can see her naked body. I'd count her stretch marks, kissing each one. I would run circles with my tongue around her nipple and listen for her moans. And I'd know when she's waking up because her legs would slowly open for me. I would go between them, kissing at her shell until my tongue finds entry. By this time her body is weakened at each lick and her pearl is revealed. She would whisper my name as if there was a room full of people but it's just me, just me tearing away at her walls until she came for me.", says Aaron.

You could see on Yani's face that she was curious as to what his tongue would feel like. Everett has been the only man she has ever been with, yet now she finds herself curious. Curious to know what another man would feel like, her guilty thoughts took her out of her elements. Again she gathered herself and asked more questions so she could get a feel of how to get Aaron and Sasha back in tune with one another and their sex life. Yani gave them some task to complete before their next session. She handed them a list of numbers for a babysitter and reservations for a night out. Yani had connections all over the city, that's why she to go to when you needed to put the spark back in your relationship. She told them once they R.S.V.P to call back to the office and set up another follow-up appointment.

Aaron kept staring at Yani; she tried her best to ignore it. Sasha was excited about the possibilities of getting her marriage back to where it use to be. She thanked Yani for listening as well as Aaron. They all stood up and Yani walked them to the door. Sasha left out first with Aaron behind her. Once Yani reached the door, Aaron grabbed her hand and caressed it. He looked at her and said "thank you", and rubbed up her forearm. Yani smiled.

"Until next time" says Aaron as he walked towards the elevator.

Yani walked back into her office and closed the door. She pushes her body up against it, slightly sinking down and says "Shit."

Yani walked over to her desk, running her fingers along the edges of it daydreaming. She thought about what Aaron said that turned him on. She herself was the perfect example of natural beauty. She slumped down in her chair, called up her secretary and asked when her next appointment was. Yani only had a few minutes to get herself together before the next couple would arrive. Now this couple had come a long way. They went from no sex to fucking like rabbits; public places and all. Now they could barely keep their hands to themselves.

Amber and Rico have been through it. Rico had come out of the military only to find Amber had been unfaithful. Rico was devastated he had planned on marrying her but they thought it was an unsolvable situation. They both thought it was best at the time for Rico to cheat to balance things out but it only made it worse. They've had their bouts with infidelity and lies, they came to Yani to try to make things right. Yani wasn't all about rebuilding your sexual relationship; she wanted you to become one with your partner on another level beyond physical. And she's been nothing short of a successful thus far. Once she finished up with that couple she headed out to meet with Lisa for drinks.

Yani hadn't spoken to Lisa since the night at the lounge.

Yani arrived at the Bistro and saw Lisa sitting in a booth; she walked over and sat down. Lisa looked at Yani with a bright smile on her face.

"Hi girl" said Lisa.

"Hey Ms. Lady", said Yani.

Lisa laughed, with that one dimple piercing the side of her cheek. Lisa and Yani ordered drinks. Neither spoke of the other night. Yani still could remember the taste of Lisa, the way she moaned and how her body swayed. Lisa, she thought about how Everett felt inside her mouth and the way Yani stared at her when she was riding his face. They looked at each other as if they were still in that nights moment, but they didn't say anything. Lisa ordered another round of drinks for them both.

"So I told Everett about what we did, although he looked disappointed, I think he was okay with it", Yani says sipping her drink, "But I loved the moment we all shared".

"It was wild girl I haven't done anything like that since college. Here I was thinking you was shy and bourgeoisie", Lisa laughed.

"Yeah we have our moments girl, Everett had fun too I think that's what I enjoy about it, it makes him happy", Yani smiled thinking of Everett.

"Damn girl yall do that all the time? Here I was thinking I was special. My girlfriend would never go for that", Lisa says drinking.

"Wait, what? Girlfiend? I thought you..." Yani stumbles.

"Girl listen I love some dick, but I also love that sweet taste of a woman so I flip flop every now and then. I'm a flopper", they both laugh as they finish their drinks.

Yani got home a little after 7pm. Everett wasn't home yet so she hopped in the shower, threw on some boy shorts and a tank top. She then went in the kitchen and made some chicken Alfredo with broccoli, one of Everett's favorites with her homemade garlic bread. Everett arrived home around a quarter till 8. Yani was in the kitchen when she heard the door slam. Everett was on the phone yelling. Yani went around to the living room to see what was wrong.

"Baby, are you ok?" she asked with worry on her face.

"Yeah, it's just work. Give me a minute baby", says Everett.

Yani was relieved. She went back in the kitchen to finish cooking.

Everett finished his conversation and walked in and kissed Yani. She still looked a bit concerned. Everett smiled relieving Yani's heart. She pulled at his beard and kissed him once more.

"You know I love you right?" Yani stated lovingly.

Everett wrapped his wife up in his arms, "Of course baby everything is going to be ok. One of the players got hurt so I have to start one of the freshmen".

"Well I know you're going to do great", Yani said issuing him one more kiss before turning for the stove.

Everett looked down at Yani's butt sway back and forth. He loved it when she cooked and did house work in her t-shirt and panties. Her colorful undies vibrantly bounced off her chocolate skin. Everett bit his lip and stroked his beard. His manhood pressed against his sweats, her tattooed body elevating his senses. He wanted her then and there, but she was cooking and there was already an incident where the fire department came out because they got caught up and forgot about the food.

...Yani was cooking for his birthday in lingerie and heels. In no time Everett snatched her from the stove and began to dismantle her body until they lost track of what was cooking in the kitchen. The firemen came, they were naked. It was just one if those things that they laugh about now...

But Everett managed to restrain himself now to avoid the embarrassment again. But he was getting turned on. Yani finished cooking and fixed their plates. Everett engulfed his food to his wife's delight.

Everett removed their plates and began washing dishes and cleaning up. Yani departed upstairs and began removing the clothing she had on, and began walking to the hot tub she knew Everett would like to relax. Meanwhile Everett cleaned; he moved Yani's stack of folders from the table a picture of one of her clients fell onto the floor. It was a picture of Aaron and his wife. But he noticed the woman so he paid no mind to the familiar face of Aaron. Everything was neat downstairs so he walked upstairs to join his wife.

Yani sat on the lip of the tub awaiting Everett. He walked over to her and stroked her face she kissed his forearm. He removed his shirt and she kissed at his stomach. She undid the draw string and pulled down his pants to release his monster. Everett smirked as Yani admired his tool. She took it in her agile hands and began to pet it like she was calming a tiger. Everett moaned as she went from petting to stroking. She sized up the head and took a portion between her lips, his head tilted back as her warm mouth heated his rod in a semicircular sucking motion.

Everett growled as she took more in letting it touch the back of her throat. He reached behind her head grabbing a fist full of locs. Yani moaned, her fruit leaked from passion, her head bounced continuously up and down. She began using her hands as saliva dripped down her chest onto her pierced nipples. She was turned on so much from pleasing she didn't care about how strong Everett's lock tight grip was, she wanted that nut. The smacking sound rained I'm Everett's ears, he grunted fucking Yani's mouth as she moaned, hands dripping with saliva. Everett roared her name he could feel his dick expand ready for explosion. Yani dripped with sensation it was enough to make her cum. But she wouldn't allow it, Everett's legs tightened as his load entered Yani's mouth.

"Mmm my daily protein", Yani joked.

They both laughed as they slid into the hot water that awaited them. Everett sat with his back against the tub and Yani took a seat in his lap, laying her head back onto his chest. Everett grabbed the medium size pink rubber band and placed Yani's hair into a ponytail exposing her neck. He wrapped up her body into his arms kissing her on the neck. Yani closed her eyes in bliss she always felt safe in his arms.

"I have to be the luckiest man to walk earth", Everett whispered.

With her eyes still closed Yani replied, "Why is that baby?"

"All the other men only get to wake up to the sun and fall asleep to the moon, but me I get to hold the sun in the day and caress the moon at night", Everett answered, "I don't know what I would do without you, I can't live without you, I've watched you grow and succeed, I mean how can anyone be more proud? I married my best friend. I love you baby. It was written in the stars and a universe was born in your eyes, I'm just honored to be your husband".

Yani clutched her eyes tight avoiding the emotions that lead to crying, "How can I be happier", tears begin to fall.

"No, no, no. None of that chump. I just want you to know what you mean to me", Everett joked.

The two kissed, Yani straddled Everett kissing him passionately and whispers, "I want to try for a baby"

Everett stared stunned as he fell into her eyes as the biggest smile began to paint itself on his face. With the water still warm Yani slides Everett inside of her. Yani gasped and looked into Everett's eyes. They began slow and steady; the water began to create small waves. Yani slowly gyrated her hips creating a rhythm with the water. She dug her fingers into Everett's skin, their eye contact strong and steady, their breaths in sync.

The rhythm increased so did the veracity of the water, it sounded as if it was applauding around them. Yani was intense and focused; with everything going on she almost forgot who had been there through everything. Everett loved her hard, sure he had his flaws but he tried to always make her day. She fucked harder the more she thought of it; she stared deeply in his eyes. Everett almost broke concentration. Her fire was blazing.

"Fuck YANI", "EVERETT", "YANI", "EVERETT", they exchanged words.

"Fuck I'm about to cum baby", Everett moaned.

"That's right baby cum for me, cum in me", Yani said fucking harder.

"Fuck!" Everett exploded.

Yani felt the warmth hit her stomach, her rhythm slowed for a second, then she rapidly stroked as she felt her orgasm reaching its peak. Everett grunted gripping her back. Yani yelled in his ear and then the room fell silent as the water also calmed. The two sat there as the water cooled them down and their breaths and heartbeats returned to normalcy.

They retreated to bed and cuddled in each other's arms. Yani snuggled into Everett's chest. Everett laid there thinking of the last time they tried for a child with all the stress of losing her father

Yani just couldn't sustain a healthy pregnancy. No matter what, Everett's comfort didn't fix it all. Yani crashed having a miscarriage she shuttered at his touch for the longest. Even with her therapeutic background she wasn't able to contain herself. It took them a while but they got back. This would be the first time things would change for the better.

"Everett I want to stop taking the pills, I'm done being scared, I want us to expand our family, I'm ready", Yani says looking into Everett's eyes.

Everett kissed her forehead, "We will baby, I think it's time that we gave it another shot".

She once again cuddled in his chest and they peacefully drifted off to sleep.

A Few Minutes

"NO EVERETT!" Yani screamed from her sleep.

Everett jumped out of his sleep, "Baby its ok", Yani trembled in Everett's arms, "What's wrong baby, talk to me, was it the accident again?"

Yani shook her head no and clutch tighter, "It was...I can't really explain it, I woke up alone and I called for you, you were nowhere near, I looked out the window to watch you walk away in the clouds".

Everett kissed her head and hugged tighter, "Baby I'm not going anywhere I promise, come on try to go back to sleep".

They drifted off again. The next day Yani saw Everett off to work, he treated her to a day at the spa. No work, no phone, just her, all orders from Everett. He arrived at work to hear even more devastating news the injured star Linebacker would be gone for the season. Everett had some choices to make. A meeting was called with all the coaches and the same name kept coming up, Makani Tachino, the true freshman from Hawaii. Everett saw the fire in him as well, he had a drive, and a motor like Everett remembered having back when he played.

"Makani, step into the office", Everett bellowed in the locker room.

The young man was timid at first then he held his head with no fear, "What's going on coach?"

"Now usually I don't do this but I have to make this decision and you're my best option. I'm moving you into the starting Linebacker position, effective immediately", Everett said rocking back into his chair, "What do you say?"

Makani didn't hesitate, "I'm ready!"

Everett smiled, "I know you are kid, you can call your family and tell them the news and see if they want to come to the game this Saturday".

"Great coach! I'll call them right away I know my sister has wanted to come visit the states and me getting the starting spot would definitely rush that decision", Makani bellowed.

"This is your chance, seize it!" Everett said with authority.

"You won't be sorry coach! I got this!" Makani dash out to tell his teammates and to call his family.

Everett rocked back in his chair after Makani left and thought of Yani. Meanwhile Yani had made it to the spa. Golden Door Spa was the place to be if you wanted the ultimate experience when it came to a spa treatment and Yani was going to take full advantage of their catering. It had a Japanese theme to it and it was a very peaceful and tranquil atmosphere. The Japanese garden scenery poured through the windows. A Yukata, which was a summer kimono, wrapped her naked frame while she sipped on herbal Thai Tea getting pampered. She felt freedom, it was a day she needed. The dream last night spooked her; she didn't want to lose Everett nor did she know what it meant. For now she relaxed as her husband instructed and let her thoughts die.

Everett picked up the phone to call Yani and then remembered he told her no phones, so he reviewed the playbook. He studied often trying to get himself ready, almost as if he was playing. Everett had aspirations of being a head coach one day. It was his father's dream to see him follow in his footsteps, but with his talent and size his father knew he was destined for more. But Everett still yearned for it, that smell of grass hitting his nose as his glasses kissed the brim of his visor as he called the shots that was his end goal. That was his dream.

Practice went along well, Makani spent most of the day scouting the more seasoned players, he learned fast and picked up things as if he was just remembering them. Everett loved his fire and he had a hit that could stun a train. He was a kid in a grown man's body; his veracity and beastly behavior while he was inside his helmet wasn't noticeable outside of it as he smiled all the time. As the final whistle blew Everett hurried to the locker room and grabbed his things, he missed his wife and wanted to make it home to her.

Everett put his car in reverse and left the facility. The music was blaring, Ron Isley hummed over the classic Choosey Lover; he let the windows down to catch some fresh air. The moon was half full and the stars were randomly painted across the sky. The leaves, even the ones that lay on the road had a gleam to them on this fall evening. An orange and purple mixture kissed the horizon and the color was slowly dissipating. Soon the city lights would be competing with the stars.

Everett stopped by Nick's to grab some takeout. He grabbed wings for himself and a spicy Caribbean salad for Yani, even though he knew she would eat his wings. After all he did treat Yani to a day of relaxation, so it was only right that he picked up some food for them both. Everett arrived home about twenty minutes later to find his wife poolside reading a book. He sat the food on the countertop and proceeded outside to where she was.

"Hey baby, how was your day?" he said.

"Hey bae, it was just beautiful!" she exclaimed.

"How was the spa?" Everett asked.

"Mighty Fine", Yani replied.

"Well that's good Ella May, but round here we like to talk a little more civil", He joked.

"You better shut up before it becomes a civil war! Now you aint gon get what I bought you", Yani growled

Everett smirked, "Yessah Miss Daisy".

Yani snorted before laughing, "You're so stupid, shut up".

"Okay I'll be good. I picked us up some dinner", said Everett.

"So how was your day, and who did you all choose to be the linebacker?" asked Yani.

"Makani Tachino" Everett said.

"I can't wait to see him in action, I'm sure you've made a great decision by choosing him. You spoke highly of him during tryouts for the team", she said.

"Yeah it's tough being a walk on but he earned it and the scholarship and I believe he has the confidence of some of the veteran players, I know the coaches believe in him and the main thing is he believes in himself", Everett added.

After dinner Everett went over his play book in the robe Yani bought him while she laid in bed reading The Cabin, a book by an up an coming author. Although the robe was too small he appreciated it. Yani fell asleep; Everett removed her glasses and the book from her hands covering her with a blanket. He laid there staring at her, thinking how perfect she was to him and how devoted she has been. He loved her passion, her nurturing ways, her inspiration and her free spirit. Everett fell asleep thinking of all the trials and tribulations they have been through together.

They woke to the sound of the alarm; Yani got out of the bed and did her daily stretches while Everett took a shower. Everett had a long day ahead of him preparing Makani for his first starting game in a leading position. Yani had to meet with Aaron and Sasha for a follow-up appointment to see how their date night went. After they both finished dressing for work they grabbed a bagel and some coffee before heading out the door.

Everett made it to the Facility and went over some things while waiting for practice to start. He still had much to do before the next game, although he felt they were ready.

"Coach E", a voice called from behind the door.

"Come in", Everett answered.

Makani opened the door, "Hey coach, my sister just wanted to thank you for the chance. She knows how much I love sports".

Everett's eyes widened it was Kai, "Coach this is my sister Kai Tachino", Makani said proudly.

"Nice to meet you", Everett said extending his hand.

"Likewise, Kani has told me a lot about you, well the school. It's all he talks about", Kai replied.

Everett smiled, "Your brother is very talented this should make for a promising opportunity".

"I'm sure he'll do you proud, my father has always loved his willingness to carry the family name proud. You're like his family now. Kani do you mind if I talk to your coach?" Kai requested.

"Sure sis", Makani said.

Makani looks at Everett, "It's cool Makani you can give us a minute", Makani left shutting the door behind him.

Everett and Kai stared for a moment then Kai spoke, "Good to see you Everett, last time our goodbye was rather rough".

Everett thought back to the debacle in Hawaii, "Yea things got carried away."

"Yeah but I enjoyed even the little time we shared, you're a special man Everett. I didn't mean to cross that line I wasn't aware of your agreement with your wife", Kai replied.

"It wasn't your fault I got caught up in the madness, I knew better", Everett answered.

"But that isn't to say I wouldn't do it again", Kai says smirking.

Everett retreated back in his chair, he hesitates then replied, "We're not going down that road again, I'm just going to get back studying this playbook".

"Well, I won't keep you but it was good seeing you Everett, I'll be in town for a while, maybe we can talk, maybe", Kai said as she walked out the door.

Everett sat flabbergasted as to what just happened, his dick stiffened at the sight of Kai, he remembered the small piece of her and he could still feel her tightness. No, he thought, not again, Yani meant too much to him, although Kai did dance in his brain. He put his head on the back of the chair and drifted off. A voice whispers "Everett", Everett jumped up but there was no one there. He felt himself slipping.

Tap! Tap!

"Coach! Coach you good?" asked Trevor, one of his players.

"Yeah. Yeah I'm good! Let's get out on the feild", Everett said as he snapped out of it.

"Alright Coach hurry up...I'm just playing, but come on", Trevor Joked.

Everett gave Trevor a look as he closed the door. Everett knew he was going to have to find a way to tell Yani that Kai was in town but he had to find a good time. Everett strived himself on being upfront with Yani and to never withhold any secrets from her. But this is not the right time; everything is all going so well. Everett put on his visor and walked out to the field.

Yani arrived at the office around 9:30, her first appointment wasn't until 11 o'clock so she had some time to get her files together and any questions she might have for her client. Yani sat at her desk, staring at her computer inputting notes in files before her phone started vibrating.

Unknown: Good Morning!

Yani was clueless as to who the caller was, she didn't recognize the number.

Yani: Who's this?

Unknown: Pardon my manners. It's Aaron. I hope you don't mind me texting you. I got your number from Kristen.

Yani was shocked. She didn't exactly know how to feel. She didn't know if this message was going to be personal or professional.

Yani: It's ok. Is everything ok?

Unknown: Everything is fine. I was wondering if I can stop by a few minutes before my appointment with you.

Yani: Will your wife be joining us early as well?

Unknown: No, just me. Sasha will be joining us at the regular time. She has court today.

Yani: Ok, sure you can come by. Is it ok if I save your number?

Unknown: On the way and of course, thank you!

Yani: Ok. See you soon.

Aaron: Yes you will.

Yani called her secretary and informed her that Mr. Webber would be arriving early and to send him straight back to her. Yani was anxious and she didn't know why, she prepared herself for

196

Aaron's arrival. Yani straightened her clothes and looked in the mirror. She walked over to the window and opened the blinds. She watered her Fichus and straightened her throw pillows on the couch. Air filled the room with an aroma from a dimly lit candle and an orange crisp scent tickled her senses. She inhaled and then released, she was mentally ready to deal with what was to come.

Pam called Yani to let her know that Mr. Webber was on the way in. Aaron walked in and Yani lost her breath.

Aaron was every bit of a man. The way his tailored suit fit his body made Yani's pressure rise. He was clean. He wore a royal blue fitted suit with a white shirt that held an accenting tie. He bore confidence. He greeted Yani with a caressing of the hand and a kiss on the cheek, it's not customary for a client to do that but she accepted it. Aaron unloosened the button of his suit jacket before taking a seat. All Yani could do was gaze at the way his pecks bulged through his shirt. Her legs tightened underneath her desk.

"So, how can I help you?" she inquired.

"I really wanted to just see you. We are always around people so I never get the time I need to speak with you." He stated.

"So is there something that you need to speak with me about?" she asked.

"Do you ever just feel something for someone that you can't explain? You know, like their mind and body is speaking to you and you have the urge to claim it", he said to her.

Yani paused, looking at him wondering what his body felt like.

"Ummm, yes! One of the reasons I married my husband", she said as if she was trying to convince herself.

"Well that's how I felt when I first saw you at your studio. And to be honest, I can't get you out of my mind", he said eagerly.

Soon after he said that he got up out of his chair, walked over to her. He then slid her back away from her desk and turned her body around, leaned in cupping her face. Yani's eyes instantly closed as his hand came into contact with her skin. Aaron took his thumb and traced her lips, he smiled in the process.

"You see you feel it too" he said adamantly.

"But..."

Yani went to speak but Aaron's lips came into contact with hers. Their tongues begin to dance. Aaron pulled Yani up out her chair not letting their lips lose contact. Her hands lay limp by her sides; he cupped both sides of her face. His scent filled her nostrils and hers into his and just when his hands were about to journey down her frame, the phone rang.

Yani scrambled to find her composure.

"Yes Pam" said Yani.

"Mrs. Cooper, Mrs. Webber is here. Would you like me to send her back?" asked Pam.

"Yes, send her back", said Yani.

Aaron fixed his clothes while Yani fixed hers. She then rolled her chair back to its regular position.

Sasha walked in, "Hello Mrs. Cooper", shocked she looks at Aaron, "Hey baby how long have you been here?"

"Only a few minutes, I came straight from the office", Aaron said but to him it felt like hours.

Yani started the session, "Hello Mrs. Webber have a seat please. So, let's get started. I gave you all a task to complete, the date. How did it go? Aaron let's start with you".

"I waited at the restaurant almost an hour for Sasha to come but she never showed up. Then I texted her she never responded. So I got pissed and I left", Aaron stated.

"So Sasha do you want to explain to Aaron why you couldn't make the date?" Yani asked.

"Well I was in court all evening; the case had gone on longer than expected. I apologized to Aaron that it had slipped my mind. I tried to make it up to him but he makes me pay for every little thing like I'm destroying his world", Sasha stated as she got teary eyed.

"She doesn't know balance. We are both attorney's but I know how to make time for my family. She acts as if only her career matters and that neither our daughter Bella nor myself matter anymore." Aaron said angrily.

"I'm just establishing myself in my field of work and I have to make a good impression if I want to be successful. Sometimes you have to make sacrifices. I love my family and I don't want to lose them, I just need Aaron to bear with me", said Sasha.

"I've been trying to get things right for almost two years", Aaron said before he walked out.

Sasha cried. Yani handed her a napkin to dry her face.

"I don't know what to do, I feel like I've given my all and he just doesn't understand. As a business woman I have responsibilities. I hate that I have to miss functions, but he does too. Why can't he see that I'm trying, I just don't think we can get back from this. What do I do now?" she said worriedly.

"Go after him. You have to fight for what matters most to you", said Yani.

Sasha didn't move. She sat there for five more minutes in silence, "We can't fix this, what am I doing? I'm being a fool. My mother told me never run behind a bus or a man because another one would be coming. I'm tired of always being the one that has to sacrifice. Aaron plays innocent but he hasn't always been the family man he says. I've caught him flirting, even texting other women. Nude photos and late night calls, I'm not perfect but I love that man. I just need to go, thank you Mrs. Cooper".

"My marriage isn't perfect, but love will win, you'll see", Yani smiled as Sasha leaves.

Yani leaned back in her chain reflecting on the morning she had thus far. She felt sorry for both Aaron and Sasha. They seemed like a great couple, but they have just grown apart in their priorities. A few hours had passed; Yani saw a few more clients and luckily they went better than Aaron and Sasha. She sat at her desk and her phone begins to vibrate.

Aaron: Can I see you?

Yani: No, I don't think that's a good idea. Are you ok?

Aaron: I really need to see you.

Yani: You should be talking to your wife; you came to me for a reason. You guys need to reconcile.

Aaron: I just need someone to talk to; I can't talk to her right now.

Yani: Aaron I just, I don't know…

Aaron: Please meet me at Empire Bar and Grill.

Yani: You can come back to the office and talk to me it's more professional…

Aaron: I'm drinking can you please meet me here?

Yani: We will be discussing your marriage right?

Aaron: Yes Yani…please come

Yani: Okay, I'll be there.

Aaron: Thank you!

Yani sat her phone down and thought about what she was doing, was this payback for Everett? Was she really feeling Aaron? Or did she just see a lost man in need of love from a woman? Sasha seemed like a good woman why were they having so many problems? Was it just on her or did Aaron have some fault? She just didn't know, she thought about Everett. She thought to text him but didn't. She went over some files and called a few clients but she didn't feel right. Her mind was everywhere she needed a clear head.

Yani picked up the phone and dialed out, "Hey Ma".

"GG, hey baby. Ms. Cynthia and I were just talking about you. Do you remember your pet pig Roscoe? Well we found a picture of you, you looked so cute with your orange cowboy hat and your pink boots", Yani's mother started.

Yani hated that name, "MA, BURN THAT PICTURE, PLEASE!"

"I'm not burning my picture. So what's wrong baby girl cuz you only call when something is wrong? Do I need to call Pastor Carter?" Ms. Diane continued.

Yani saw just how country she was after spending all this time in California, "No Ma, well yes, I don't know…"

"Okay, Cynthia get me Pastor Carter number", Ms. Diane called out.

"No Ma I mean something is wrong, but it isn't", Yani said catching her mother.

"Well baby you gotta pray, that's all you can do. I love you, hear me?" Her mom says.

"I love you too Ma", Yani sighed.

"And tell Everett I love him I know he miss my cooking and when yall gonna have me a grandbaby. I aint getting no younger", her mother questions.

"Bye Ma I'll tell him", Yani chuckled a bit as they hung up.

Yani grabbed her things and prepared to exit the building it was a bit of a drive to Empire, and she had to beat traffic.

Practice was still going on and it was getting late. Everett stood out on the field with his arms crossed, he surveyed the players. His thoughts on Makani were right; he had the mechanics to be a great player. But today he felt distant from the field; his thoughts of Kai poisoned his brain. He hadn't heard from Yani but attributed it to a busy day at work, but still he missed her, so he sent her a text.

Everett: Hey baby, having an off minded moment, I miss you...

Yani looked down at her phone to see Everett's name pop up as she sat across from Aaron.

"What did you need from me Aaron, why are we here?" Yani asked.

"I needed more time alone with you, ten minutes just wasn't enough. I know I have this thing going on with my wife but I just can't get you out of my head", Aaron answered.

"Where would we even go from here Aaron? What would we ever be other than an affair? I'm not leaving my husband and its clear your wife loves you, what can I do for you other than cause us both pain?" Yani snapped.

Aaron is a little drawn back, "So have thought about us?"

Yani jumped as he grabbed for her hand. Yani thought to reach for her phone as she saw a missed call from Everett, but hesitated as she looked at Aaron. What was she doing here, it wasn't right. She barely touched the food she ordered but finished the glass of wine. She had to go. She leaped from her seat and stormed towards the door.

Aaron reached in his pocket and pulled enough money to cover the bill and tip. He chased Yani to her car and caught her before she got in.

Meanwhile Everett worried it was late, he called the office and her secretary stated she had left. It wasn't like Yani he thought and after so many calls he got in his truck and went to look for her.

Yani stood at her car, her back was pressed against the side, Aaron stood about 6'1" she didn't have to look up as much as she did with Everett.

"Why did you storm out, what's wrong?" Aaron questions.

"This is wrong Aaron", Yani said looking down.

"What? This?" Aaron said as he kissed Yani.

Yani pressed against his chest for separation but his body made her arms buckle until she fell into him. It was passionate; he spread apart her legs and reached between her thighs playing with her fruit through her panties. Yani moaned as she leaked. She gripped the back of his head. He pushed her panties to the side as inserted his large fingers. Yani began to grind on his fingers until she started to cum, "Everett", Aaron stopped. He removed his fingers and pulled away. Aarons face grew cold as he stood there.

"Are you serious", Aarons face scrunched up.

"I can't", Yani said turning away.

Yani jumped in her car and fumbled for her keys. She found them and sped off, her thoughts were jumbled, she wasn't thinking, her brain was elsewhere. The blazing of horns flared loudly, she had taken her eyes off the road. She began to panic. She pulled over and began to hyperventilate. The thoughts of her crash attacked her psychological state. Headlights flashed by her eyes. She screamed. She heard screams, a familiar yell.

"Everett help me", Yani whispered praying.

Her phone began vibrating, it was Everett, "Baby...hello...baby, please...where are you at?" Yani was talking so fast he could barely understand her, "Baby slow down".

"It happened again, Camille. Something is wrong with Camille, I can't get her out", Yani reached for the passenger seat belt only to find air.

Everett wiped sweat from his face, "Baby breathe it's gonna be okay, Camille is gone remember? Count with me and breathe"

"1...2...3..." they counted in unison.

"Okay baby, now tell me where you are", Everett asked.

Yani gave her location and within minutes Everett arrived. He pulled Yani from the car and held her tight. She cried into his chest, Everett locked her car doors and carried her to his truck. Everett was quiet; he hadn't seen her like this in a while. He turned on the air and rubbed her back and tried to calm her breathing. They arrived at the house. Everett carried Yani inside and laid her on the couch as he fixed her some tea and grabbed some things to help soothe her breathing.

"I'm sorry I didn't mean to..." Yani started.

"No baby, no it's ok, long as you're ok", Everett held her tight he was worried he had lost her again.

No matter what, he would fix it, it didn't matter what it was or who it was. He would fix it. He made a silent promise to Yani as he held her. Although his thoughts wandered he didn't risk sending her into a further stressful state, so for now he let it go.

The Forbidden Fruit

Everett looked over at the clock it was 5:30 am, his thoughts wondered. He looked at his wife who finally slept peacefully, "what made her regress", "Something had to spook her", "Something just wasn't right". He questioned himself as he quietly crept out of bed. He threw on his sweats and a hoodie. He walked down stairs and then quietly out the door. He stood on the porch; the cool morning dew from the wind grasped his bearded face. He threw in his ear buds and pulled his hood over his head. He started down the paved middle section of the yard; he unlatched the gate and then closed it behind himself. He passed his down the street neighbors who were riding their bicycles and an older man who was walking his dog as his stride picked up. After a while he removed his ear buds and let mother nature doctor on his spirit. The crickets chirped as his legs kept moving. He came up on a park that he and Yani spent much time. The park was 3 miles from their house; he didn't realize he had come so far.

The sun had now stretched over the sign "Dalani Park". He started down a small man made path that curved just at the end. He placed his large hand on an oak tree that had two initials carved in it, "EC & YS FOREVER"; he softly stroked it as small parts of tree bark crumbled at his fingertips. Beyond the tree he saw water, his ears filled with the sounds of a babbling brook, the smell water flared in his nostrils. He envisioned Yani staring at the stream in her lotus position as he carved their names in the tree. It was a peaceful time then, she had come into her own after being almost mentally lost. But he was there and wouldn't leave her side.

When he first got the call about the crash his heart dropped. Her mom was on the other end going hysterical and his first thoughts were that Yani was gone. He and three other players rushed to the nearest hospital, Yani was unconscious with tubes hanging from her body. Everett had to be detained with much force as doctors were trying to do what they could but he wasn't satisfied until her brown eyes were looking into his. Camille's mother had come to identify her, she and Ms. Diane wept in the middle of the hospital floor. There wasn't a dry eye in the waiting room as painful screams rained through the hallways. Everett hugged them both trying to be a solid foundation when at the time it was hard to stand.

For two days he sat and waited for a response. He read a poem as tears dripped down his face, his eyes were red and his voice scratched as he pushed out every syllable. He kissed her forehead and begged for her to just speak to him. He hadn't slept in days. His head lay on her abdomen as he prayed. He had spoken to his father who wasn't feeling too well himself, but he told Everett she had to fight the battle, there was nothing he could do, he had to let Yani be strong. He looked around the room as blurry images of balloons and flowers filled his vision, he then laid his head back down catching a glimpse of the locket Camille's mother wanted her to have. A small hand caressed his head as he had drifted off to sleep. His eyes lit up as Yani's tear-filled eyes looked at him.

Everett called for the doctors to come; he almost picked one up and carried him to the room, "She's awake!" The doctors rushed in to check on her as Everett ran down to get Ms. Daine.

A text goes off interrupting his thoughts…

Yani: Baby where are you?

Everett: Hey, I'm sorry, went for fresh air I'll be home soon…

Yani: K, I love you

Everett: Love you more

Everett arrived home as Yani finished up her shower. She sat in a robe not looking like her usual self.

"You ready to talk about it?" Everett asked.

Yani paused, "I was scared".

Everett folded his arms and leaned against the dresser, "Why? What happened?"

"I...I don't know. I wasn't myself. I saw lights coming my way and I got confused and I panicked. It took me back to the accident...Camille...I miss her", Yani stumbled as she clutched her locket.

Everett strode over and seized Yani, "I can miss the game baby I don't have to be there".

"No you will not, I'll be fine baby, I promise", Yani forced a smile.

No matter how much Everett pleaded; Yani wouldn't let him miss a game. She kissed him and told him she would come to the game if she felt up to it. He accepted that and left her to rest while he got ready. He left the house, when he got the end of neighborhood he texted her one more time.

Everett: I love you; you mean the world to me.

Yani: I love you more. Get that win baby! Go Trojans!

Yani laid there after she replied to Everett, she went down her text message history and saw the messages from Aaron; she thought to text him. She wanted to explain about the other night. But she erased the feed and placed her phone down. She closed her eyes for a split second before her phone went off again; she thought it was Everett so she jumped for it.

Aaron: We need to talk

Yani hesitated then put the phone back down, until it vibrated once more.

Aaron: Yani, please.

Yani: You have to stop texting me.

Aaron: Just once more Yani, then I'll be out of your hair.

Yani: I apologize for last night. It was a mistake this can't happen…

Aaron: You feel it or you wouldn't have even responded in the first place

Yani paused thinking about Aarons touch…

Aaron: Don't you?

Yani: You're missing the point we can't do this, too many people can get hurt just by what we've done already

Aaron: Yani please

Yani placed her phone down gripped her hair as 4 more messages came in.

Aaron: Yani

Please don't do this

Yani I'm begging

Just see me, that's all I ask

Yani: ...okay, but this is the last time Aaron, where do you want me to meet you?

Aaron told her of a spot they could meet and talk quietly. Yani bathed herself and threw on sweats and a t-shirt, her hair was in a ponytail and she put in her gold hoop earrings and walked out the door. She then realized her car was still on the side of the road. She thought to call Aaron but didn't want him knowing she was home alone. She called Lisa who luckily was in the area. When Lisa picked Yani up she noticed she wasn't herself.

"Are you going to game?" Lisa asked.

Yani quietly answered, "No, I have a lot on my mind just going to chill at the spa".

"Oooh girl I'll go with you, we can get our..." Lisa started.

"No, not this time I just need to be alone", Yani says cutting Lisa off.

They pulled up to the car and with a kiss on Lisa's cheek Yani gets out. She cranked up her car and drove to meet Aaron. The whole drive she thought about the events that had occurred the other night. She wanted to get this over with. She pulled into the mini shop and got out. Aaron was there waiting sipping on a milk shake which he got an extra one for Yani. She sat down although his advance for a hug was noticed.

"What did you need Aaron?" Yani said abruptly.

"You!" Aaron said reaching for her hand.

"You know what..." Yani stood up leave when Aaron caught her arm.

"Wait, please let me just show you something", Aaron pleaded.

Yani followed him into a clothing store. The place was nice, she loved clothes. She thought of herself as a fashionista. Aaron took her over to rack and pointed out a brand she wasn't familiar with.

"It's beautiful, I don't know the designer", Yani marveled.

"My wife was once happy and ambitious, now she's just power hungry, she created this line in school and had much success, she just quit for law school", Aaron said handing her one of the garments, "Try it on for me".

"I don't think I..." Aaron kissed her in mid-sentence and pushed her into the dressing room.

He ripped her shirt and delicately sucked at her nipples. Yani did her best to silence herself but his mouth was pleasurable. He used his hand to push her sweats and panties down. He massaged her clit as she braced herself against the wall.

Yani tried to push his hand away but his fingers only found entry to her berry. He massaged her insides as if they were a delicate blossom, she couldn't resist so she hoisted her leg up so he could have better access. Aaron lips found hers once again; Yani accepted kissing him back fervently.

Aaron removed his fingers, gliding it passed her clit. He took one of his fingers and traced her lips with her own essence before kissing her. Her taste was savory; he took his fingers sucking away the excess. Her flavor relapsed off of his tongue as if she was his addiction. Aaron fell to his knees, sitting Yani on the dressing room bench throwing one of her legs across his left shoulder. Now lips were upon lips, she bucked against the tenderness of his soft lips proceeded by a gentle suck.

Yani put her hands over her mouth muffling her moans; her body twitched at each suckle Aaron left on her body. Aaron loosened his belt, undoing his slacks. He stood up, his slacks dropping to the floor freeing his fully engorged penis. He scooped Yani up and at the same time he positioned himself on the bench with Yani in his lap. Yani felt his thickness press against her; she was caught in the moment. Aaron lifted Yani up and slowly eased her down onto him, she felt him expand inside her.

The intensity of each stroke caused her to moan. Aaron pulled her close as he dug deep. He kissed at neck and nibbled on her ear lobe.

"How does it feel?" he whispered.

Yani tried to answer but the words for the pleasure she was feeling didn't exist. Aaron kept stroking as his mannerism demanded an answer. The deeper he stroked the more he became imbedded in her texture. Each stroke felt like therapy to her, they were skin against skin. Aaron throbbed inside her; he massaged her essence as he expertly navigated her ocean. Yani's body began to convulse, so Aaron pumped harder.

He felt Yani releasing all over him, her muscles contracting around his manhood intensely, it was driving him wild. Aaron grabbed Yani's ass digging his fingers in her skin as he released himself inside her. He collapsed into her neck, sucking it as his dick pulsated and released every bit of him that have collected for the last couple of months. Yani tried to get up but he held her too tightly.

"What did we just do!" she said worried and exhausted.

Aaron just stared at her beautiful face, sweat dripping down her brow. Yani got up looking for her panties and sweats. Once they were on she remember that her shirt was ripped she couldn't leave the store like this. Aaron finally got up putting his boxers and slacks back on, not taking his eyes off Yani.

"Wait right here, I will get you another shirt." He told her.

"Ok" she replied.

Aaron came back with a V-neck t-shirt. Yani took it out his hands and pulled it over her neck.

"Look Aaron we both are married, this should have never happen, we should've never let it get this far." Yani stated.

"But you felt what I was feeling since our first kiss, so how could we not?" said Aaron

"Because we are married", she said but to him that was more of a question than answer.

She didn't wait for his answer she left for her car. What would be a minutes' drive seemed like an hour. She ran in the house and jumped in the shower. She stood under the water, letting it drown her face to mask her tears. She scrubbed her body trying her hardest to remove Aaron scent; still she saw flashes of him in the moment. Even though she regretted it she loved it. She scrubbed even harder at the realization of her enjoyment. Yani got out the shower throwing on her terry wrap, laid across the bed and drifted off to sleep.

Back at the game Everett's heart thumped as Makani took the fumble in for another touchdown. He really did run like the wind. Everett ran down the sideline to meet his freshman with a chest bump. The atmosphere was amazing; the only thing missing was the blown kiss from Yani. Everett turned back towards the field, the offense converts a 3rd down and sets up for a touchdown.

"Alright coach let's bring it home", one of the other coaches roared.

Everett called a huddle, "Okay men listen up and look around you. These are your brothers; this battle is fought and won with defense. Tie game, I want that ball, go get me that ball. On three, Team. One, Two, Three".

"Team", they all say in unison.

"Defense", the head coach yells.

Everett crossed his arms and studied the field. The defense ran out and set up, the ball was hiked and a deep throw landed the opposing team in the red zone. Everett's heart dropped as his players began bickering about the missed coverage. Everett saw something he never expected. His young freshman took ahold of the situation and made sure they were back into the game. The opposing quarterback got under center and hiked the ball the big bruising tailback swallowed the handoff in his clutches. He thundered his way through the defense breaking tackles as the hole to the endzone opened up. Everett's heart raced, until the booming collision jarred the ball loose. One of the cornerbacks picked up the ball and took off for the endzone with Makani and the others blocking his way. Everett looked up to see where the hit came from. None other than number 2 Makani made the thrashing hit. The stadium rocked and the field was stormed as the clock hit all 0's. They retreated to the locker room it was buzzing.

Everett stepped into his office to have a moment of peace. He loved football and after every win he hugged the picture in his office of his father. The second thing was to call the woman responsible for him getting back in the groove. Yani. So he pulled his phone from his pocket and called.

Everett called Yani; the phone rang a few times with no answer so he called once more. When he called the second time she answered right away, "Baby, we did it, we won! ...I know ...I'm happy too... Thank you so much, you got me here no matter how many times I say it, you got me back here. I'm going to gather a few things and then I'll be on my way home, I love you"

"I love you too..." Yani hung up.

Everett made his way to the car; he parked in the dark corner of the lot under the shade. It was hot so he tried to keep the car cool. He was still hype about the win; he had some pep in his step. He pressed the button to unlock the door when he heard his name, he turned to see Kai. She was dressed down in some cotton shorts and a tight crimson shirt, with gold writing, her hair was pushed back in ponytail and a hat covered her hair. Her auburn skin glowed; a full Samoan sleeve covered her left leg. She wasn't as thick as Yani and her tone was definitely lighter, but she had a sex appeal Everett just couldn't deny.

"So Everett, how have you been?" Kai said walking towards him.

"I've been good, enjoying football and...and marriage", Everett stumbled on words.

"There's nothing to be afraid of Everett, See I'm all alone Makani took off with a few teammates which leaves me with nothing to do", she said walking up to him.

Her scent filled Everett's nose, he gulped, "Look this is not a good idea".

"What? This here?" she grabbed his dick through his pants and began stroke it, "Come on just let me suck it".

"No, no you can't do this. I mean it's still people around. I mean this is wrong", He says pushing her back.

"I'm sure they don't care and its dark no one would even know what happened to you", Kai says convincingly.

Temptation grabbed at Everett's hand and he released his grip. Kai kneeled pulling down his sweats and took Everett into her mouth, he laid his head back. Kai contracted him into her mouth until he touched her throat. But she took it further. Everett groaned with delight, grabbing the back of her head. It was sloppy; he heard the slurping in his ears.

"No, no stop", Everett said.

Kai looked up as his face turned serious, "What's wrong?"

"This, us being here, it's wrong I love my wife I can't do this", Everett answers.

Kai stood up and kissed him, she pulled him around to the hood and mounted his dick after pulling down her shorts. She gasped as she felt his thickness fill her. She fucked him hard her juices running down his dick. His phone begins flaring he could tell it was Yani by her ringer.

"You got to stop", Everett says lifting Kai off of him and answers his phone, "What's wrong baby? ...Ok, I'll bring it...I'm just talking to one of the coaches, ok, I love you too".

"What the hell is wrong with me this is wrong, you are wrong, I'm damn sure wrong. Kai we can't do this shit no more. Like dead ass, you and I can't have contact. Do you know how serious things got in Hawaii, imagine if she caught you here", Everett blurts.

Everett pulled up his pants and said his goodbyes to Kai; she told him where she would be staying. Everett knew the place but brushed off that he did. He flew home after stopping to the store to bring Yani ice cream. Everett shook his head thinking what in the fuck did he just do. He couldn't do that again he smelled of Kai. He pulled into the driveway and walked upstairs with the ice cream for Yani. She was lying watching a movie. Everett kissed her forehead and gave her the ice cream. Then he took off for the shower. He stood in the mirror shaking his head, how could he have been so stupid. He turned on the hot water and quickly washed off Kai's scent.

He felt a small face touch his back; it was Yani, "Hold me please". Everett held her as Yani allowed the water to mask her tears once again.

Everett held her; he wanted to take her away from everything. He kissed her deeply on her frontal lobe as their bodies made contact. The water didn't matter. Infidelity wasn't an issue. Outside interference wasn't even on their radar. It was about them and only them. Everett took her face gently, he looked into those brown eyes and confessed his sins with his smile to her; she partially smiled back as she traced his lips before kissing him.

Everett and Yani fiddled with each other's hands as they laid there. Yani's lip pulled in then pushed out a few times. Everett knew it was something on Yani's mind but she wouldn't say anything, even if he asked. She had to take her own time to do so. Everett removed his hand from Yani's to her displeasure. Everett stood up and opened the curtains sweat pants adorned his lower half as his shirtless upper body glistened with tattoos. Yani folded her arms pouting. She wanted him to get back into bed.

"What's wrong sugar pop", Everett joked.

Yani raised her lip and eyebrow at Everett sneering, "You know I hate when you do that".

"Well you know I'm going to keep doing it, Chocolate Mango Berry Sugar Muffin Cake", Everett continued.

Yani unfolded her arms, "E I'm warning you, I said stop"

Everett turned from the window towards Yani, he placed his hands on his knees, "Aww snooky woo..."

Yani leaped towards Everett as he dodged her, taking off down the hall he gripped the wall and turned down the corridor that connects the family room with the kitchen. He placed his back against the wall listening for Yani's footsteps.

"Oh Everett", Yani called.

Everett stayed quiet, "Come on baby I just want to talk to you"

Everett heard the cocking of a toy gun that shot Styrofoam arrows. Everett snuck for the laundry room where he hid the reserve weapons

Yani wasn't aware of. Yani crept threw the house. She had on a sports bra and spandex shorts, her hair was in a ponytail and she had removed her socks for traction. Everett emerged from the laundry room with two toy guns like an assassin in search for Yani.

"Everett baby help", Yani cried wolf.

Everett stood stuck not knowing whether the cry for help was legit. He crept around and peeped from the corner to look for Yani.

"Baby help", she said once more.

This time Everett got concerned, "Baby where are you?"

"By the bedroom hurry", Yani called back.

Everett rushed to check on Yani but he wasn't going to be fooled so he kept his guns drawn. Yani lay there holding her knee; Everett dropped his guns and came to her side only to get shot in the chest.

"Hmm seems like I win", Yani giggled uncontrollably. Everett's face was priceless, "Aww baby you were really worried", Yani said as she lifted herself from the floor.

She tiptoed and kissed Everett who still stood there confused on how he lost. Yani looked back and smirked, "Chump".

Everett dashed towards Yani; she took off for the room probably wasn't the smartest move since there was no escape. Everett caught her by the bed tackling her onto it. The force of the landing broke the wood of the bed frame and the bed hit the floor. The couple was shocked then fell out laughing. Everett got up to assess the damage and it was unfixable.

Yani laughed, "Damn killa"

Everett chuckled, "Uhh fuck you very much, that was both of us".

Yani stood on the bed, "Come on does it look like this frame could have done all that damage?"

Everett bit his lip, "Get your ass down, we have to go to the store".

"Come here there's something on your back", Yani said as Everett turned around.

"What?" Everett questioned.

"Me!" Yani leaped onto Everett's back.

He laughed as he carried her into the bathroom. He turned on the shower then dropped his sweats, "Me next", Yani joked lifting her hands.

Everett lifted her sports bra and her breast fell into form. He then bent down coming face to face with her pearl as he slipped off her shorts, "Don't try nothing now, we gotta go", Yani teased.

Everett popped her on the butt, "Get in".

"Ouch, you ain't my daddy", Yani said rubbing her now sensitive cheek.

"Oh yeah?" Everett asked.

"It hurts now, kiss it please", Yani pouted.

Everett bent and kissed her flesh, "Better?"

"One more", Yani pleaded.

Everett obliged, "How bout now?"

"Yep. Thank you daddy", Yani smirked as she got in the shower.

They hurriedly bathed and got dressed. Everett threw on his sneakers and basketball shorts, with a tank top and a fitted cap. Yani's body adorned a white and black sundress, with stripes. She wore sandals, her hoop earrings, her bracelet and a sun hat with her big sun glasses like she was ready for breakfast at Tiffany's. It was a hot day so they took the convertible. Yani removed her hat and sat it in her lap. Everett had a bye week and Yani took some time off, so the couple enjoyed a weekend to themselves.

Yani looked over at Everett; he had one hand on the steering wheel and the other lay on the arm rest. His beard glistened in the sun from the Shea Oil Yani rubbed in it earlier. His tattooed arms and chest made Yani's mouth water. She was turned on by the visual. She looked down at his lap wondering if she should have some fun. His basketball shorts had come up a bit over his knee near his thigh. Yani relished in the thought but resisted.

Everett caught Yani staring and licked his lips. He felt pulsation between his thighs. Catching a glimpse of her protruding nipples through her dress, he bit his lip. The store wasn't far but he felt like pulling over and giving her the business right then and there. He pulled into a parking space in front of the furniture warehouse and they got out. They walk through the doors and were greeted by a few smiling faces. They were introduced to LA, she was an interior designer. Yani loved her from the start, especially with her name she figured she knew what she was talking about.

LA extended her hand shaking theirs as introductions were exchanged, "So Coopers follow me this way".

LA was tall, about 5'9", she had medium curves and long legs. She had a mocha tone with a short haircut, her eyes were a light brown and her full lips accentuated her complexion. Yani looked at her breast pour from her blouse. A tight black high-waisted skirt hugged her lower frame. Everett peeped his wife's demeanor and knew what it meant, she wanted LA.

They sat down at her desk and she pulled up the design program, "Okay first off Yani I love your hair, geeze you are beautiful. Excuse me for the lack of professionalism but I love black natural beauty and black love, look at you both. King and Queen."

Yani and Everett blushed at her enthusiasm. It was genuine though, so they accepted it. Yani locked eyes with LA. She was sure that LA was into women but she didn't want to seem rude, so she sat back and admired. Everett just watched as his wife stalked her prey. He enjoyed it and reaped all the profits.

"So Mr. and Mrs. Cooper what are we looking to do?" LA inquired.

Yani leaned forward, "Well you see we were playing this morning and my giant of a husband broke the bed."

Everett laughed at the accusations, "So Yani you had nothing to do with this?"

Yani stood up as how she had done on the bed earlier, "Look at this frame, does it look like I can break a bed?"

"Mmm...I mean I will be more than happy to help you...with the bed...well you know", LA stumbled on words trying to catch herself.

"Okay what do you have to offer", Yani asked flirtatiously sitting back down.

LA bit her pen and turned the computer screen around, "How about this nice California King, it's soft and plush, and full of room".

They both hung on her words, LA looked at Yani's nipples, which had now fought their way to being seen again, "So I can set this up for delivery today and be there with you when they deliver it. I'm very thorough and hands on with my clients and their needs".

Yani smirked, "We'd be glad to have you over to our home; maybe you can stay for dinner and dessert."

"We'll have to see about that", they paid and shook hands then departed to go to the grocery store and sex shop, Yani needed some things.

Yani and Everett went to *Smith's* a local adult store that was mostly for couples. Yani grabbed something special for the evening. They then stopped by the market, Yani was going to cook, they arrived at home around 4:30 p.m. Everett got the bags out of the car while Yani went inside to cook. She wanted to cook something savory tonight, so she decided on filet mignon with red potatoes and asparagus and for dessert a strawberry parfait. Yani was very systematic when she had her eyes set on something or someone and she wouldn't stop until she got what she wanted.

Dinner was done, so Yani went to the bathroom to freshen up. Everett was in the living room playing the PlayStation. Sometimes Yani and Everett would play together; it was always a competition with them but always in fun. Yani came around the corner in an all-white cat suit that she picked up from the sex shop. Everett eyes widen at the sight of here.

"Damn baby!" Everett said sitting straight up in the chair.

Yani just smiled and walked past him, her ass jiggled with each step she took, "You like it?" she said turning around in slow motion.

"Damn right I do", Everett said biting his lip.

She went back in the kitchen and checked on the food she was preparing, everything seem to be to her liking. It was nearing 7 o'clock and the delivery guys should be pulling up any minute now. Everett got up and turned off the game. He then turned on the stereo system and the surround sound so the tunes can be heard within the entire home.

The doorbell rang. Everett headed to the door to see who it was and it was the delivery guys. Yani saw LA pulling in the driveway in a Range

Rover. Everett led the men back to the room to switch out and set up the new bed. Yani held the door for LA to come inside, welcoming her to her home. LA admired the black art that adorned the walls, especially the ones of her and Everett. Yani told LA to have a seat, sitting next to her. LA then gave Yani the delivery documents to sign to complete the sale of new California King Size bed.

"Thank you", Yani states.

"Well I do aim to please", LA said winking.

"We might have you design a baby room for us", Yani smiled.

"Oh my goodness you're pregnant I can't even tell!" LA exclaimed.

"No not yet but we're definetly giving it a shot", Yani replied.

"Well you already have a Hollywood family go ahead and add a beautiful baby to it", LA stated.

"That's the plan hopefully she or he doesn't get Everett's ears", Yani laughed.

"No disrespect but girl your hubby is fine", LA said as she snapped her fingers.

"No not at all girl and thank you!" Yani exclaimed.

The guys came back around about twenty minutes later; Everett thanked them and saw them to the door. Yani insisted that they go eat; LA watched Yani as she got up from her seat and proceeded to the kitchen. Both Everett and LA watched Yani's ass bouncing by in synchronized motions. They were mesmerized by her curves. Yani called them to the table for dinner.

"So LA are you married?" Everett questioned.

"No not yet my girlfriend and I are just chilling as they say. But it's not near that serious yet; we still do our own thing. We actually met at a swinger's party", LA said moaning as she took a bite of her food.

Yani's interest peaked, "Well we've been together for eight years, a little more if you include college".

"Wow, nice", LA started, "I bet you guys were wild in college".

"We did our thing, we might show you one of our videos one day", Yani blurted out.

"Videos, I thought you deleted them", Everett raised his eyebrow.

"Well I'm glad she didn't I would love to see you guys in action", LA blushed, "It must be this alcohol talking".

The conversation grew quiet as they finished their meal. Once they were done Yani offered up dessert. She cleared the table and told them she would bring the parfaits to the living room. Yani joined them not long after with the dessert and a can of whip cream. She handed LA and Everett theirs, she then asked if they wanted any whip topping. Everett declined but LA said yes. Yani leaned over to spray the whip cream on the parfait when it went all over LA's chest and lips.

"Damn I'm sorry; let me clean that up for you, "Yani apologized. Yani sat the whip cream on the table and stood in front of LA and leaned down, "Let me get that."

Yani ran her tongue down between LA's breast, Everett sat staring at them. He could feel his blood beginning to boil; he ate his dessert fast licking the bowl clean. Yani moved her tongue slowly down to where the buttons on LA's shirt began before going back up to lick her lips. Their tongues began to swirl and Everett watched Yani's ass dance to the beat of the music. Yani stepped back until she was in the middle of the floor, the music took over her body. She swayed left, then right, running her hands along her frame; she put on a show that the two loved.

Everett felt his rod stiffen and press against the seams of his pants. LA sat there biting her lips as she enjoyed the show. Yani moved in once again, this time she unbuttoned LA's blouse. Her red pushup bra ran over, so Yani gathered up her breast in her hands then into her mouth. She exposed her nipples, running circles around them with her tongue. Everett sat there admiring his view while he stroked his manhood through his slacks.

"Stand up", Yani said to LA.

LA stood up; Yani turned her around so she could get her fully undressed. Yani unzipped her skirt slowly, and as her cold hands begin to run across LA's flesh she let out a slight gasp. Yani then told her to sit back down. She then took to her knees and spread LA's legs apart. Her tongue ventured slowly between her thighs, when it finally made contact with her bloom, LA's head fell back into the couch. Everett tried to keep his composure, but these two tigresses were making it hard for him, very hard.

"Damn!" Everett said aloud.

Yani sped up pace knowing that it was making Everett feel some type of way. You could hear the muffled moans that escaped the pillows that grace LA's face. Everett got out of his chair and crawled up behind Yani. He then pressed himself against her, she leaned back looking up and invited him to her lips to have a taste of LA. They lingered for a few moments before she dove in back between LA's legs. Everett stroked at Yani's back, grabbing her locs. He was feeling the urge to be within Yani, so he tore at her clothing, ripping her cat suit way. Yani was turned on by his aggression, so much that she attacked LA even more, she inserted two fingers and ate away at her flesh.

Everett ran his fingers between his wife's legs, tasting her. He then placed his fully erect penis against her as she leaked faucet, he plugged her with all his girth. He stroked her intensely as he yanked at her locs. Yani moaned and groaned in delight as she creamed all over her husband's dick.

Everett pulled out to taste her just to ram himself back inside her again. Yani's back arched up at her surprise entry before finding its resting spot again. LA suggested that they go try out the new bed, so they got up and the girls went ahead of Everett hand in hand.

Everett grabbed the can of whip cream and headed back to join them. When he arrived the girls were already at play. He took the can and sprayed the cream on LA as well as Yani. He instructed them to lie still because he had dessert to finish. The girls complied. Everett took to LA, running his tongue around her nipples, down to her navel, he parted her sea and licked away the whip cream.

His tongue found entry to her insides gathering up all her flavor until he managed to have her give him every drop she has within her. She laid there in defeat. Then it was Yani's turn, he started at her floret, he reached her navel then made his way to her breast he squeezed them together and sucked on her nipples. He put his gears in reverse and headed back down until he reached her gardens entry. He plucked at her petals, dug at her soil, and withdrew all the moisture she had left. She also succumbed to the beast.

Everett pulled Yani to the edge to the bed, standing up he filled her up and pumped vigorously until he too reached his demise. Before they knew it they all collapsed in the bed and were fast asleep. Yani woke up the next morning to a note on the night stand that read…

"Hope you enjoy your new bed as much as I did. See you again soon, LA"

Yani smiled and laid back down next to Everett. They had plans on going to Disney Land for the weekend, but they opted to stay inside, locked in their room, to enjoy the sweet sounds of one another.

The Beginning of an End

It was a bright October morning Everett looked at Yani as she lay across his chest; it was past noon according to the cable box.

Everett pushed Yani's locs back and kissed her forehead, "How she felt about making breakfast?

Yani wanted anything to take her mind off of Aaron, how could she do it. She's never lied to Everett. Her mind was lost; Everett kissed her bringing her back to reality.

"You ok baby? Everything is going to be ok I promise", Everett said rubbing the sides of his wife's arms as she stood in front of him, "Let's cook".

"As long as you don't make the pancakes", Yani joked it was the first real smile she had in a few days.

Everett smirked then picked his wife up and carried her around. He then slams her on the couch and they begin play fighting. Everett blew wet air into her stomach making a farting noise. Yani giggled saying, "What are you 3", so Everett tickled harder. Yani laughed uncontrollably. Her giggles warned his heart, Kai was nothing more than a memory at that moment.

Everett kissed Yani's navel, "I can't wait until I can do this as our daughter..."

"Or son!" Yani snapped back smartly cutting him off.

Everett chuckled, "Okay, okay or son is growing in your beautiful stomach. You think I'll be a good father baby?"

Everett laid on Yani's stomach, "I think you're going to be a great father", Yani says caressing Everett's head.

Everett pulled up and kissed Yani; he sat her up and began nibbling at her thighs. Yani's eyes closed she took herself back to their first time, when she was fresh. She felt his tongue roll over her flesh, the colors of pink and brown swirled in her head. She felt her yoni tighten up. Everett licked softly; his passion was so gentle it turned her on. Yani felt it. She felt him giving her his whole attention like the first time they made love.

Yani felt warmth, her legs tightened, her nipples stiffened. She moaned his name, "Everett", she grasped his ears, "Everett", her thighs gripped his neck as she felt that burning build, "EVERETT", she came. She pushed it out, the orgasm she felt so long to have again. Her body jolted. She shook, convulsion after convulsion. Everett pulled up and wiped his face.

He sat down with his back to the couch. Yani pulled herself from her dormant state and mounted Everett. She kissed him passionately, "I love you", she said as she let him into her passage. Yani lifted herself up and then back down, repeatedly, slowly as she looked onto his eyes. His girth filled her aching needs. Sure they've fucked to the point of no return. But the love. The love making hadn't happened in a while. She missed it, her body moved up and down as she cradled him into her bosom. Tears fell from her eyes as she felt his penetration in every recoil.

Everett dug into her back he felt her nectar seep down his shaft. He pushed deeper into her making her gasped, "Oh my God", Yani's body heated onto his. They traded breaths. Everett locked her into his arms. He wouldn't relinquish his grip. Yani's body quivered. Everett's head swung back.

He unleashed. He unleashed everything he had in him. Yani's stomach warmed. Her body went limp; her head fell into his shoulder. Everett wrapped her into his body. A torrent of tears fell from her eyes and kissed Everett's back.

He felt their warmth and held her even tighter than before. Even though Everett just felt himself fall in Yani's grasp once again Kai momentarily crossed his mind. He was trying so hard to shake her but she just wasn't letting up. Yani stood up and peered into Everett's eyes and kissed him on the forehead. She headed to the bathroom to clean herself up. Everett sat on the couch and awaited her return.

Everett and Yani still had to be to work so they had a quick breakfast, "I promise next time we will at least get breakfast started", they both giggled and got dressed for work.

Yani saw Everett out the door as she put the finishing touches on her outfit; she was in a much happier space than she's been in the last couple of days. Yani hopped in her car, let down all the windows including her sunroof and turned up the radio. Her smiled shinned brighter than the sun itself. At every red light men stared and honked their horns to try and gain her attention, she just smiled and dismissed it.

Yani arrived at work, but before she even went into her office her secretary stopped her and told her that the Webber's were inside waiting on her. Yani couldn't think her once elation quickly went away.

"Are you ok Mrs. Cooper?" her secretary asked.

"I...I'm fine." Yani said with a grim look on her face.

She slowly made her way to her office door, inhaling deeply as she went inside, she could hear the couple arguing back and forth.

Yani sat her things down and positioned her things in her chair with a grim look on her face, "So, how are you guys?"

They both tried to speak at the same time, one trying to blame the other for their now troubled marriage.

"Since our last session, nothing has changed. Aaron is constantly on me about how much time I spend at work. He doesn't understand how it feels to be in a field dominated by men. I'm trying to make a name for myself. I'm trying to help be a provider for my family. I come from nothing and now everything is within my grasp and I just need him to understand how much I need this." Sasha said wiping her eyes with the tissue Yani gave her.

"And how do you feel Aaron?" Yani asked avoiding eye contact.

"Well it's like this, I love my wife. I love her, but I also need her. I know the amount of work involved in building yourself up, the amount of time and dedication it takes. I am a black man that has made it out of the hood, and out of the stereotypes of society. I own my own law firm. I've rubbed elbows with most notable people in the city." Aaron stated

Yani intervenes, "My experience being a black woman, a business woman in a world dominated by men I can understand the want for support. My husband Everett has done everything he could to support my dream. And I believe that is why I am where I'm at now. Sometimes we just need understanding because we have goals too."

Aaron sneers at Yani, "But at the end of the day none of that matters if I don't have a family to come home to. I support my wife and everything that she does and everything she strives to be, but enough is enough. Our daughter needs her mother and I need my wife", Aaron turns to Sasha, "Until you are ready to make sacrifices I can't be with you."

"You can't be with me? Who have you become?" Sasha got up and ran out crying.

"Sasha wait", Yani yells out as the door slams.

Aaron didn't move, he just sat there staring at his hands with his head down. Yani could tell that he loved her, she felt bad for him, she was blinded by her care for Aaron that she neglected Sasha. She got up from her chair even though hesitant and sat next to Aaron. She inhaled his scent slowly; she loved the lite smooth aroma. She took her hand, rubbing Aaron on his back telling him everything would be ok. Aaron just shook his head while he pulled away from Yani.

Yani reached for Aaron, but he moved away and started pacing. He still hadn't said a word since Sasha ran out, he couldn't understand how she couldn't value a man like him.

"Aaron you need to go after her", Yani said.

263

"I'm sick of this shit she needs to change", Aaron growls.

"You can't just give up on your marriage Aaron", Yani says trying to console him.

"How could she not see, what is having everything if you have no one to share it with?" he said with desperation in his voice.

"Sometimes we neglect the things we need; sometimes we have to lose something of importance to realize how much it really meant to us." Yani explained standing up walking towards him.

Aaron drew back from her, looking deeply into her eyes and asked "why can't she be like you? What am I saying; I'm talking to the woman I want about the woman I'm married to, this just doesn't make any sense".

"What doesn't?" Yani questioned.

"I think I love you", Aaron said as he surprised Yani with a kiss.

"What do you mean you love me? Aaron think about this. We can't, I know that you are going through problems in your marriage but this isn't the answer. We are both married, we just can't", said Yani pushing him back.

Aaron heard every last word she said yet he kissed her again, Yani tried to pull away but Aaron became more aggressive. Aaron grabbed her and hemmed her against the door locking it. He squeezed her tight as they engaged in a deeper kiss. Heavy breathing and panting was heard as their hands wildly caressed one another. Aaron begins to remove Yani's blouse, sucking at her neck kissing each spot more passionately than before. His hands traveled through her locs, drawing in her coconut oil as he breathed her in. He unbutottoned his shirt and undid his slack exposing himself, sitting back in the chair.

Aaron pulled Yani on top of him drawing her breast out of her bra, placing one in his mouth. Yani's head tilted back in the pleasure she was being given. Aaron eased her skirt up exposing her lace thong panties and ripping them away. Her moist flesh rested against his thickening manhood. Yani felt his pulse between her legs, throbbing and growing in size. He placed both palms on each of her cheeks and brought her body closer into him, he squeezed as she got closer. Aaron then grabbed her by her waist lifting her up so that he can grow to full extension before easing her back down onto him.

Yani gasped as Aaron gained entry. Slowly he assisted her in rocking back and forth until all of him was inside her. Aaron gawked at her, he sucked on her supple breast, licking each nipple. Yani's head rolled back high off this moment. Aaron picked Yani up, walking over to her desk and gently laid her on top. Yani's body stretched on top of the oak wood. Her body flushed under the desk lamp, enhancing her ink.

Aaron hands traveled her frame, as each stroke drove in her harder and deeper. His legs begin to unravel beneath him, as he was nearing orgasm. He thickened and throbbed inside her wet kitten, her milk spilling onto him. He lost complete control when her big brown eyes met his; he leaned in one last time filling her bowl up with every drop he had left in him. Slowly he pulled away, not losing contact and helped her back up. They both got dressed without saying a word about what just happened. Yani opened her desk drawer and pulled out a compact mirror making sure her mascara hadn't smear.

"I know this is wrong, but you feel so right!" Aaron said before walking out the door.

Yani's thoughts swarmed, what happened to her? Everett's betrayal didn't soften the blow of her actions. A married man? A client? This couldn't happen anymore she had to tell Everett. She looked at the couch a small puddle hovered above the spot where she and Aaron fucked. She grabbed the leather cleaner and pad from her cabinet and scrubbed until her tears wet the material. She collapsed on the floor and rested her head on the cushion.

She wanted Everett, she wanted to look in his eyes and confess her sins as if he were her religion. She picked up her phone and called to no answer. She attributed it to him being at practice but she left a voicemail anyway.

"I know you're at work...I was just missing you...I know things have been crazy lately, but we've made it through worse...Just call me when you get this, I love you"

She looks down at her phone to an incoming message:

Aaron: I love you...

Le' Art of Fucking Up

It was nearing the middle of the season and Everett just wasn't the same. He drew back his arm throwing a balled up sheet of paper with plays he drew up. He just couldn't get it together. His mind was everywhere; he looked down at the picture of Yani and picked it up. He caressed the outline of her face; he slouched in the chair letting his head hit the back of it as he looked up. He placed the picture on his chest and thought. He hasn't been the best husband; there was a time when he was lost in alcoholic bottles, no job, bills due. But he had Yani, she never let him down. What in the fuck was Kai doing in his head? He thought.

His brain turned until he drifted, he felt a warm sensation of lips touch his face and a hand grace his lap. He thought it was a dream until he woke up to find Kai staring at him. Startled he dropped the picture and cracked the glass. Kai covered her mouth saying she was sorry. He picked up the photo and placed it back on the desk. Everett then backed up in the rolling chair pushing himself away from her. Kai smirked removing her top, her nipples stared at Everett. He looked at the door then back at Kai. His face grew bashful as his dick swelled. She reached over pushing Yani's photo flat. She dropped to her knees and pulled for his manhood.

"How, how did you get in here?" Everett asked nervously.

Kai got up, locked the door and turned back towards him, "There's no need to be scared just let me take care of you".

She pushed him to her lips, Everett grunted, "No stop, don't do this".

"She won't know just calm down, let me give you a massage", she replied.

She engulfed him, using her tongue to lick away the precum. She spit and slurped, motioning her hands in a twisting form. She pushed his legs apart and tasted his sack. The thickness of his dick lay on top of her face as she sucked at his flesh. She moaned, as the sounds of wet smacking kissed Everett's ear. He grasped her head and began fucking her throat until she gagged. Saliva shined and polished Everett's vessel. He lifted her up and tasted her nipples. Her skin was fruit flavored, mango. He clutched at her ass removing her shorts.

Her pussy dripped with anticipation she thought of him being inside her since Hawaii and the last time that was abruptly interrupted. She turned around and eased herself onto him in reverse. She threw her hair over her left shoulder to the front. She arched her back and slowly took him inside of her. She moaned and whimpered, her tightness clutched his wood. She maneuvered herself up and down, creaming against his flesh. Her whimpers called for him as he watched her back trail.

She leaked on his shaft as it filled her insides; he then let the chair down to the floor level. Her hands rested on his thigh as she braced herself for the thrusts. She look back at Everett, he bit his lip as his large hands gripped her sides. Her back art began to shine as she started to perspire. Everett looked down and watched as his thick rod spread her.

"Fuck me", she whispered leaning back against Everett's chest.

Everett lifted her up and placed her on his desk. He pulled his swollen manhood from her insides and showed her. She engulfed as much as she could between her lips, sucking then licking every inch, then she laid back flat on the desk. He pushed his way back inside of her, placing one hand on her hip and the other rested beneath her breast. Gripping one he bends and takes her nipple in his mouth as he stroked. His aggressive strokes rocked the desk dislodging the draws slightly.

She gripped Everett's arm and grinded against his flesh. Everett grunted as he pumped away, she moaned excepting every thrust. She pulled herself up by his arms, wrapped her arms around his neck and her legs around his waist. Everett grunted as his legs weakened she came all over him. He knew it and felt himself getting close. She pulled in tight moaning in his ears until he released and they fell out.

Everett looked at the clock and began to lose his mind, he was supposed to be home for dinner with Yani. Kai used his personal bathroom to clean herself off, he followed behind her. Kai began cleaning herself then looked down at Everett's dick, his tip still dripping with cum.

"Missed a spot", she says dropping down sucking him clean.

Everett groaned, "I got to go Yani is going to kill me".

He lifted her up and they get dressed. Everett looked around to make sure everything was in order, but in his haste he overlooked Yani's protruding red panties from his desk drawer. Nevertheless Everett walked out and checked to see if the coast was clear, they left and he made his way to his car. He looked down at his phone 4 missed calls and 6 text messages. Everett didn't know what the fuck he was going to do? He threw his phone, it vibrated once more and a message came through it was of Kai, "It was everything, I enjoyed you and I look forward to the next time". Everett began to lose it.

He turned off his phone and pushed it between the armrest and the seat. He pulled up to the house and sat in the truck trying to think of what

274

he would say. The situation had become too much for him. He beat at the steering wheel and contemplated everything and to turn off his phone was even more uncharacteristic. He was wrong; he knew karma was nipping at his heels. Fearful of an argument he crept into the house. Yani sat at the table with her arms crossed.

"Where in the fuck have you been?" Yani screamed.

"Baby calm down, something came up", Everett said in defense.

Yani stood up, "Are you fucking serious? I called you and texted you multiple times. I called Coach D and he said everyone was gone but your black ass".

"Baby I don't even have my phone just calm down", Everett said reaching for Yani.

"Don't fucking touch me, E, I swear just get the fuck out of my face", Yani's fists began to ball.

Everett backed off as Yani began puffing. They just stood there in silence. Everett felt small even though he towered over Yani. After five minutes Yani broke down, her knees hitting the floor. Everett walked over lifting her up. After she punched him a few times in his chest, she cried into it. For the first time he cried too. What in the hell was he doing. This shit wasn't right, in his office? What if somebody walked in? He took Yani upstairs and laid her down. He went back downstairs and cleaned up. She made dinner, how could he do her like this, he thought. His fury grew as he slammed his fist against the counter.

"What's wrong E?" Yani asked.

Everett turned he thought she was sleep, "I don't know, things are getting out hand. I need to fix this".

"What? What's getting out of hand E?" Yani questioned.

"Nothing let it go, it will be ok. I just gotta fix it", Everett brushed it off.

"Something is bothering you, just come to bed. I'm not mad, I was worried", Yani said calmly.

Once upstairs, Yani and Everett got into bed and drifted off to sleep. Yani tossed and turned all night, she couldn't seem to find a way to get comfortable. Once she finally started to rest she was awaken to a ringing sound. She saw her phone sitting on the night stand lighting up, she turned and looked to Everett's side of the bed to see what time it was, 3 a.m. Yani picked up her phone and it was an incoming call from Aaron.

"What's wrong baby, who's that?" asks Everett.

A nervous look comes across Yani's face, "No one baby, go back to sleep", she says.

Yani put her phone on silent and text Aaron.

Yani: Don't call me!!!

Aaron: Please, we need to talk. Can I see you?

Yani: Aaron, what we did was a mistake. I never want to see you again. Don't ever call my phone again.

Aaron: Yani, I need you right now. I love you.

Yani: DELETE MY NUMBER

Yani sat her phone back on the night stand, turned over and wrapped her arms around Everett. She couldn't get herself to fall back asleep; tears begin to fall from her eyes. Everett turned facing her, not noticing that she was crying and kissed her on the forehead. Eventually Yani managed to go to sleep. She reached out for Everett but he was gone, looking at the clock she saw that it was 10 a.m. She reached for her phone and saw that it was 5 missed calls, all from Aaron. "What have I done she thought to herself."

"You ok?" Everett said standing in the doorframe.

"Yes" Yani said sitting her phone on the bed face down.

"Good, a package came for you", Everett said holding a box.

"Who is it from?" Yani questioned.

"I don't know somebody with the initials AW", Everett started reading the card as Yani's heart dropped, "A token of my appreciation, AW"

Yani's eyes widened as he pulled a pair of pink diamond earrings from the box, "Oh those are nice".

"Nice? Damn, I'm in the wrong profession. Who's AW though baby?" Everett questioned.

Yani thought quick, "An old Miami client...um he and his wife own like a big jewelry company down there...umm...they make the rappers custom piece babe, you know that".

"Oh, yeah. I forgot. But you sure you okay? You look worried", Everett said out of concern, "Come let me take care of you" he said as he led Yani to the bathroom.

Everett had drawn a hot bath, lit candles and prepared a fresh glass of pineapple and strawberry juice. He stood behind Yani, gathering all of her locs in his hand and put them in a ponytail. He then slipped the straps to her night gown off her shoulders watching it drop to the floor. Yani turned around and faced Everett, standing on her tippy toes and kissed him on his nose. She then got into the bath as he sat behind her joining her. He grabbed a sponge, soaking it and let the water drain onto Yani's body, she leaned back into him in delight.

He picked up some fresh strawberries from the glass and ran the fruit across Yani's lips. "Turn around and kiss me" he told her. The kiss was full of passion, and promise. It was as if they had confessed all their immoralities in a kiss and was given forgiveness. Everett stroked Yani's face reminding her of the love he has and the love that will always remain.

She looked him deep in his eyes as tears began to form. She knew from that moment she needed to tell Everett about Aaron, "Baby, I...."

Before she could even get the words out her mouth they were kissing again. Everett washed Yani's body from head to toe making sure he didn't miss a spot. He rinsed her body and his as well before stepping out of the tub and grabbing a towel. He instructed Yani to stand there while he dried her off. Once he was done he wrapped a towel around Yani and walked her to the bedroom. He laid her on their bed drying whatever water was still left on her body. He then went to the dresser and grabbed the mango butter.

Walking back over to Yani he looked at her and smiled. He rubbed the butter on Yani's body kissing it in the process. Yani was in heaven, but Everett was enjoying this much more than her. He loved catering to her, it was his pleasure. Yani's phone started vibrating so she sat up grabbing it while Everett stood in front of her. She was face to waist with him. She looked at it. I need to see you was in all capital letters. "Who is that?" asked Everett.

"Umm, who's who?" Yani stumbled.

"Who is that saying I need to see you", Everett questioned:

Yani's heart dropped, "It's just one of my clients baby they're going through some things and needed to see me".

"Oh okay it better be cuz I aint scared to knock somebody out bout my GG", Everett joked as he flexed.

Yani sat with her head down not speaking, "You sure you're okay?" Everett questioned.

"Yeah baby my bad let me get ready to handle this client", Yani said as she collected her thoughts.

"That's cool just let them know you have your own sex therapy to get back to", Everett smirked as he popped Yani on the butt.

As Yani walked into the bathroom, Everett sat on the bed questioning her behavior. It wasn't like her not to laugh or show anger, especially at the mention of the nickname GG. He didn't know what to think but he trusted his wife. He just didn't know what caused the change in her mood.

Yani grabbed the box and looked at the earrings. What was Aaron thinking sending this shit to her house? Was he crazy? He knew Everett might have the chance of seeing it. Yani looked at the earrings and felt nauseous. How long could she keep this up? And he kept telling her he loved her.

No, she needed to end it before it could go any further. She knew one thing, she loved Everett, Aaron was nothing more than an infatuation.

Take the Good with the Bad

Yani nervously sent a text to Aaron and told him to meet her at her office, while Everett got dressed for work. Yani sat on the bed she just wasn't feeling like herself. She blamed it on the stress and pulled out something to wear into the office. It was a brightly color wrap dress and some heels. From the bathroom Everett watched in amazement. She just was everything he wanted in life. The big game was tonight and he had to mentally prepare. Yani would be there and he hoped Kai wouldn't be.

Everett pressed Yani against the car and kissed her, her knees felt weak as she caved into his arms. He hadn't melted her in so long but she felt his strength. It held her even after he let go. Everett kissed her forehead and walked to his truck. He left in the direction of the stadium and Yani went towards her office. It took her about 20 minutes to get there from where she lived. She turned off the CD player and let the top down. Her locs blew freely in the breeze. She felt freedom begin to build in her as she knew what she had to do, the sickness lessened.

Yani pulled up into her parking spot and got out, her secretary was gone on vacation so she had to open the place up. She went in and sat down at her desk and caught a glimpse of her and Everett at the first football game he coached. They lost but you could never tell that by their faces. He was happy to be back with football and it made her happy because it made things more pleasant. As Aaron was buzzed in he walked up to Yani smiled and reached for a hug, only to be told to sit down on the couch. Aaron smacked his teeth and sat down.

"No, don't touch me", Yani snarled.

"What you didn't like my gift?" Aaron sat confused.

"Don't send shit to my house, are you stupid?" she snapped.

"What is your fuckin issue Yani, or doctor or whatever the fuck you want me to call you?" Aaron snapped.

Yani calmed herself, "Aaron listen, this little thing we did was a mistake go home to your wife. If you fought as hard to keep her as you fought so hard to be with a married woman, maybe you wouldn't have this issue".

Aaron laughed, "Were you a married woman when you were cumin all over my dick?"

"Listen like I said it was a mistake it will never happen again", Yani said as she tried to remain calm.

"That's what your mouth is saying, your body would tell me a different story, I know you love me too", Aaron rebuts.

Yani calmed herself once more, "Aaron I called you here because I wanted to end this face to face, I am a very personal person and right now I'm personally asking you to leave".

"So I guess you're husbands is finally pleasing you again huh?" He snapped.

"Keep my husband's name out of your mouth and worry about your wife", Yani fired back.

"You've wanted to know what my wife has been experiencing from day one", Aaron said cockily.

"Get out", Yani mumbled.

"Excuse you?" Aaron questioned.

"I said, get the fuck out!" Yani exploded.

"Fuck you Yani", Aaron fired back.

"No fuck you, why are you still here?" Yani snapped.

Aaron stood up and walked over to Yani, he pulled out his stiff manhood, "Because I know this is what you want, go head suck it"

"You must have lost your fuckin mind, get away from me", Yani said as she pushed herself back.

"Oh no?" Aaron questioned. He lifted Yani up and put her on the desk, he pulled the side tie of her dress and it opened. He started to eat at her floret his lips felt soft against hers she felt herself losing the strength to fight then she felt his dick press against her entrance.

"Dammit I said no!" Yani slapped Aaron with all her might, "Get the fuck out Aaron and lose my fuckin number and never come here again".

"Fuck you Yani, I ain't the only who did dirt you're just as fucked up as me. But Karma is a bitch", Aaron said before leaving.

Yani fixed her clothes and broke down and the rain begins to beat against the window. She stood up and walked over to the window and looked out thinking.

Steady were the drops of rain, and the pain that was being expelled from her eyes. The guilt was getting to her. How could she ever be so stupid to jeopardize her marriage? How could she ever be so weak to let someone come rip apart what's been held together for so long? Yani wrapped her arms around her body, wanting to be held. She started crying angrily, throwing books off her shelf before sitting down in her chair, searching through the mess looking for the Webber's file. When she located it she started ripping it, before placing them in a shredder.

She wanted to be rid of him. She then deleted his number from her phone and erased all the messages that were exchanged. Yani needed to get herself back, she needed to be who she always was and not what she's become. After removing everything about Aaron from her personal space she felt a little weight being lifted from her. Her once weeping eyes dried up. She relaxed just a little bit. She knew she had to tell Everett she just didn't know when and how. Everett trusted her, valued her and she couldn't bear the thought of losing him, ever. She picked up the books and straightened her office back.

Yani got herself together mentally before heading home to get ready for the big game tonight. She knew Everett was super stoked about it and that she couldn't wait to be there in the stands cheering him and their team on. She called up Lisa and asked if she wanted to come to the game. Of course she agreed and told Yani she would be on the way as soon as she got dressed.

Yani threw on her class colors, white shorts, and her sneakers. She then put her locs in a ponytail, tying a ribbon in her hair like the old college days. She was ready for the game. She grabbed a backpack and packed it with a hand towel, some water and fresh fruit. Everything seemed to be in order, she is about as ready as she could possibly get.

Everett was sitting in his office going over the playbook when he heard a knock at the door.

"Come in" he said.

"What's up sexy!"

"Why are you here Kai?" he questioned

"I'm here to see Makani play and to see if you and I can play before the game", Kai said walking towards him, locking the door once again.

"No, are you stupid? I don't want you here, my wife will be here." Everett said standing up from his chair.

"It won't be the first time your wife and I will be in the same place with you", Kai said with a smirk on her face.

"You flew 2500 miles for some dick, using your brother as an excuse?" Everett jolted at her.

"Are you serious, I didn't even know you were his coach in the beginning", Kai said.

"But you are still here, yet talking to me and not watching him, what's up" responded Everett.

"Don't get mad at me because you're unhappy with your marriage. I knew this back in Hawaii when I first met you. I knew I could have you when I wanted you!" rebutted Kai

"Are you mental? You know what, get out!!!" he said pointing to the door.

Kai started to speak but Everett interrupted her.

"Get The Fuck Out!!" Everett screamed.

Kai stormed out the door slamming it behind her, almost shattering the glass.

Everett composed himself, the game was about to start in about an hour and a half. He grabbed his playbook and headed to the locker to meet with the players and coaches. Everett walked towards the locker room, when he sees Kai and Makani laughing.

"What's up Coach?" ask Makani.

"Let's go Mr. Tachino" Everett says to Makani while giving Kai an evil look.

"What's that about?" Makani looks at Kai confused.

"I don't know; guess he's nervous about the game. Go on, make us proud Kani!" Kai said as they embraced in a hug.

Everett ran out on the field as if he would be strapping up to play. He looked up to the box office and blew kisses to where Yani was sitting as he did every game. It was game time he looked down and saw Kai sitting near the student section and gave her a sneer. Then he focused on the game, he wasn't about to let her ruin his night.

"Makani come here", Everett yelled.

"What's up coach?" Makani answered.

Everett slapped him on the shoulder pads then grasped the sides of his helmet, "You know what time it is right? Take everything out of your mind and focus, I need you today, I want that ball every time you see it! No games, I put you here for a reason! I know you're going to make me proud!"

Makani was hype! Sure enough on the second play Makani took the ball for a defensive TD. Everett was so into the game he almost got a penalty for running on the field. Meanwhile up in the sky box Yani and Lisa were screaming until their voices grew horse. Yani felt dizzy, she grasped the chair and sat down. She grabbed the water out of her purse thinking she just needed to calm herself down. She clutched for her mouth and ran for a trash can.

"Girl what's wrong?" Lisa asked.

Yani continued to throw up, then it subsided and the nausea returned. Lisa told her maybe she should go home and lay down. Yani didn't want to leave but the constant nausea proved to be too much so she agreed to leave. She tried calling Everett but she remembered he lost his phone so she called one of the other coaches. The message got to Everett and he took off for his car, he looked over at Makani and told him to remember what he said. Everett made it home a few moments after Yani and Lisa. He ran upstairs Yani looked pale. Everett lifted her up and told her they were going to the hospital. Yani knew when it came to her health Everett didn't play the radio. So they rushed to the emergency room.

Yani was curled up under Everett waiting for the doctor. He looked up to see the game on the television. Everett's eyes lit up as he saw Makani intercept the ball and take the ball down to the 1 yard line. The first play was stuffed and they loss 3 yards. The second play was an incomplete pass. Yani held Everett's hand and told him it would be ok. The ball was hiked and handed to the running back. He was stuffed for a second time. But it was a trick play as the quarterback scored on the sneak. Everett's heart level rose as people cheered in the waiting room.

"Congratulations baby", Yani whispered, Everett kissed her on the forehead and thanked her.

"Giyani Cooper", the nurse called.

They got up and Lisa waved as they walked to the back. Yani was instructed to take off her clothes and put on a gown. After a few minutes the doctor walked in with the nurse.

The doctor shook Everett and Yani's hand, "What seems to be your symptoms Mrs. Cooper?"

"I've been nauseous, light headed and I haven't been feeling like myself", Yani explained.

"It is flu season. Have you been having any aching or sweats?" the doctor asked.

"No I have had a slight fever", Yani adds.

"Well we're going to run a few test and get you all fixed up", the doctor said smiling.

"Okay", Yani said as she pushed out the words.

Yani smiled through sickness, it made her happy to see that it was Everett still there taking care of her. Everett kissed her and lifted her onto the bed. Nothing else mattered to either of them they were in blind blissful love. The nurse came in and drew blood for the test. Yani gave blood samples, urine samples and got an IV in her arm of 0.9% sodium chloride for hydration. To have as many tattoos as she had, she hated needles. So Everett held her hand through it.

They sat there as they waited on the test results laughing about old times. It was comforting, something they had been missing over the past few weeks. The doctor knocked on the door and came back in. The couple sat there as the doctor made a joke and they all laughed. It seemed like he was a Cal graduate so the win tonight didn't make him too happy and he let Everett know about it.

"Mr. and Mrs. Cooper, congratulations you are having a baby", the doctor said with a smile on his face as he shook their hands.

"We did it baby!" Everett yelled.

"I want to do an ultrasound to see how far along you are", The Doctor said.

The doctor pulled the machine over to Yani, "This is ultrasound gel and it will be a little cold".

The doctor pointed to the embryo on the monitor. He turned up the sound, and for the first they heard their baby's heartbeat.

"Looks like you're about 6 weeks, I'll leave you two to celebrate", He said printing the picture of the ultrasound.

Yani's heart dropped as she cried, Everett had a mix of emotions this was the best night of his life. He stood up and started to cry, he was so happy. He looked up wiped his face before he kissed Yani. He told her everything will be ok. Nothing was going to stop them this time they were going to be a happy family and have a beautiful baby.

"Everett..." Yani started.

"What's wrong baby is something hurting, do you need me to go get the doctor, I'll bring his ass back", Everett joked, "No, Seriously what's wrong baby?"

Yani swallowed and took a deep breath, "Everett there's something I have to tell you...I've been with someone else..."

301

The Breaking Point

(Excerpt from Surviving the Storm)

Everett sat at the bar of the hotel he had been staying at for the past two weeks. He took a couple sips and tried to clear his head.

"Hello are you Everett?" the stranger asked.

"Yes, can I help you?" Everett responded.

She walked closer, "Well Everett, it's more like I can help you. See your wife was my husband and I's therapist."

"Listen I don't get involved in her work business and if you don't mind I'm kinda going through some shit right now", Everett snapped.

Sasha smirks, "Well Mr. Cooper as I was stating, I want to help you. You see the man you seem to be swallowing that drink over is my husband. I caught the messages between them. They've been extremely intimate with each other. This is him".

"So you're telling me this is the dude that has been sleeping with my wife and he's your husband?" Everett snapped.

"Yes", she responded.

"Where in the fuck is he?" Everett yelled.

"I don't know but he's usually at work on Osmond and 22nd, Weber and Associates Law firm", she timidly responded.

Everett's tempered flared as he recognized the face from the party at the house and the photo on the table. He chugged the last bit of his Hennessey and storms out of the hotel lounge. He left without giving Sasha time to respond. Everett blindly drove to the address. There was a black truck parked by the sidewalk. There was no time for a subtle entrance so he busted through the door of the firm as he looked for Aarons office. He searched rooms until he found it. He bypassed his secretary and pushed through the door to find Aaron at his desk with his head in his hands.

"What the hell are you doing here?" Aaron screamed.

Everett's fist were balled, "You motherfucker, you were in my house! What kind of man are you?"

"Get the fuck out before I call the police!" Aaron howled.

"Not with your fingers broken motherfucker", Everett roared.

Everett took off towards Aaron; he lifted him up slamming him through his desk after taking two punches. The two battled as fist flew and things broke.

Aaron's secretary showed up after hearing the commotion, "Get off of him! I'm calling the cops!"

Everett mounted Aaron and began punching downward until Aaron was unconscious. Everett's hands were swollen as he got up and stumbled towards the door like the Hulk leaving wreckage behind him. The secretary shook as Everett walked pass her. His shirt tattered and covered in blood stains. His heart thumped, his adrenaline raced. Everything was blurry.

Everett jumped into his car and sat just when his phone rung, it was Yani. He ignored it. She called again and Everett could hear the police sirens in the background. He finally picked up but remained silent.

"EVERETT!" Yani yelled.

"Did you fuck him in our bed? Aaron, did you fuck Aaron in our bed?" Everett questioned.

"E what did you do?" Yani began crying.

GET OUT OF THE CAR NOW!...

50638903R00180

Made in the USA
Lexington, KY
23 March 2016